THE
WILD ONES

MOONLIGHT BRIGADE

THE
WILD ONES

MOONLIGHT BRIGADE

C. Alexander London

PHILOMEL BOOKS

PHILOMEL BOOKS

an imprint of Penguin Random House LLC
375 Hudson Street, New York, NY 10014

Copyright © 2016 by C. Alexander London.
Map and interior art copyright © 2016 by Levi Pinfold.
Penguin supports copyright. Copyright fuels creativity, encourages diverse voices,
promotes free speech, and creates a vibrant culture. Thank you for buying an
authorized edition of this book and for complying with copyright laws by not
reproducing, scanning, or distributing any part of it in any form without permission.
You are supporting writers and allowing Penguin to continue to publish books for
every reader.

Philomel Books is a registered trademark of Penguin Random House LLC.

Library of Congress Cataloging-in-Publication Data
is available upon request.
Printed in the United States of America.
ISBN 978-0-399-17100-0
1 3 5 7 9 10 8 6 4 2

Edited by Jill Santopolo. Design by Semadar Megged.
Text set in 12.25-point Winchester New ITC Std.

To the squirrels in my yard who attack my tomatoes:
I know what you're really up to.

Part I

THE SONG OF ANKLE SNAP ALLEY

Chapter One

MUSKY MO HEARS THE MUSIC

BRIGHT leaves fell from tired trees, and day by day they browned on the forest floor. Cool air sharpened its bite and nipped at the skin of any animal who hadn't begun to thicken his fur or fortify his feathers. Winter was on its way.

On a riverbank near the giant city of steel that the animal folk called the Slivered Sky, a gang of otters had gathered, huddling to keep warm, while the brittle ground crunched below their claws. They sat in front of a traveling coyote, who had an old tin-can guitar strapped to his back.

"If you think this winter will be cold, let me sing you a song of the real winters in the Howling Lands, where the sun shines but gives no warmth, where the lakes freeze over thicker than a turtle's shell, and a sneeze shatters when it hits the ground. These are the hungry winters and a fella without supplies surely goes cold and dies."

The coyote's voice was scary and soothing at the same time. It slid from his tongue like gravel coated in gravy. The otters held one another's paws as they listened to him.

"You ever sneezed an icicle?" the coyote asked.

The otters shook their heads no in awed silence.

"Want to hear a song about it?"

The otters nodded their heads yes.

No one had ever seen this gang of otters this quiet before. These were the Thunder River Rompers, twenty in all, and they considered themselves the toughest, tightest, and most terrible of all the river otter gangs around.

Weren't they the ones who knocked over the big beaver dam three seasons back?

Yep, sure as sunshine, they were.

Weren't they the ones who chased off a full-grown hawk just this past summer?

Everyone knew they were, especially that frightened hawk.

Weren't they the gang that rumbled and raised a ruckus with any passing creature, and considered themselves the only pals o' the paw worth palling around with anyway?

Yep, that was the Thunder River Rompers, best of brothers and brawling-est of beasts.

So why were they sitting here, drop-jawed and wide-eyed, listening to some mangy coyote tell a tall tale instead of pounding him into the dirt, flaying his fur, and using his pelt to cozy up their riverbank holts?

That was the question their leader, Musky Mo, put forward with a snarl, just as the coyote was about to start his song.

"I could use a coyote-fur couch this winter," Musky Mo said. "Looks mighty warm to me!"

The coyote sat back on his haunches and looked the leader of the otters over lengthways and long ways and up ways and down ways. He had a smirk on his gray muzzle and a devious twinkle in his eye. There were scars that cut through the brown-and-gray fur on his back, and he wore not a stitch of clothes.

Even the otters, freer than any folk, wore wrist cuffs woven from seaweed and green knit watch caps with their gang insignia emblazoned on the front: a terrible otter claw bursting from a frothy river, a fish in its fist.

They also wore glasses, every one of them, because when otters were on land, they were nearsighted.

Once, a passing skunk shouted that the Thunder River Rompers were more like Thunder River Rubes. The skunk had a good stinking laugh over that, because a rube was a foolish fellow. Musky Mo, never one to let an insult pass, dragged that skunk into the river and held him down so long, he washed the stink right off him. No one ever disrespected the Thunder River Rompers after that.

But the coyote didn't seem to care a whisker for the Rompers, or Musky Mo's reputation as a drowner of skunks. He'd stepped from the dark brush and settled himself in front of them without so much as a "beg your pardon," and then he'd offered to start singing songs like the riverbank was his very own turf.

Musky Mo was not having it. "So how about you get up out of here, coyote, before I make it so you can't never get up from anywhere again."

Coyote liked his winter song and *did not* like to be interrupted when he was about to sing it. Confronted with Musky Mo's demand that he "get up out of here," the coyote licked his lips.

"I didn't mean to bother you fine fellows," Coyote said, the gravel in his voice getting rougher. "I know you otter folk have a lot of ruckus to raise before winter sinks her teeth in. I'm only a weary traveler seeking some rest and some good company. I'll be off shortly. But first, perhaps, might I sing my song?"

"You're not welcome here," Mo grunted at him, flexing his webbed front paws for a fight. "And none of us want to hear your howling. Right, boys?" He grimaced to show off his otter fangs. The rest of the gang stood up behind him and grunted.

Coyote was bigger than all of them, but grossly out-numbered. He sighed as he swung the guitar off his back. "Why don't I play you just one song before I go? It's a short song."

Musky Mo laughed when he saw the guitar. "You ain't got no strings on your guitar," he said, pointing. The other otters laughed along with their leader, because indeed, the coyote's tin-can guitar didn't have a single string on it. "What good's a guitar without any strings? It won't make a sound!"

"Well, you best listen closely, then," the coyote said, and began to strum the invisible strings. The otters stopped laughing and furrowed their brows at this strange coyote. Perhaps he had Foaming Mouth Fever? He wasn't actually foaming at the mouth, but he was acting stranger than any canine the Thunder River Rompers had ever come across.

The coyote plucked and played his stringless guitar with passion, closing his eyes and tapping his back paws, nodding along to a tune that only he could hear.

After a moment, he opened his eyes and looked at the dumbfounded gang of otters. "Ya like my song, boys?"

"We don't hear nothin'," Musky Mo grumbled.

"Listen a little closer," the coyote said. "I wrote this song for you Rompers, after all."

The otters leaned forward to listen closer, bending their thick necks and lowering their little heads toward the guitar. Their tiny ears twitched in anticipation of the music.

The coyote looked down at his audience and adjusted his grip on the musical instrument . . . and then he turned it around and smashed its heavy end down onto Musky Mo's head!

He flattened the otter's face into the cold mud with a *splat*, then swung the guitar along the line of other otters, knocking them into one wet otter heap.

"*Ooof! Ooof! Ooof!*" they grunted.

Musky Mo tried to get up and grab the coyote's tail, but the coyote jumped away, tossing his stringless guitar as he spun. The guitar knocked three more Thunder River Rompers back into the mud, and the coyote landed behind Musky Mo. Before the otter could turn around, the coyote lifted Musky Mo off the ground by the scruff of his neck and faced him toward his own gang.

The otter's paws scrambled uselessly in the air, and the coyote grinned through clenched teeth. Musky Mo's eyes widened as his gang froze in place, unsure how to help their boss.

The coyote shook his head ferociously and flung Musky Mo head over tail into the Thunder River.

"Swim away, Musky Mo!" the coyote yelled after him. "If I see your furry face again, I'll turn your bones to toothpicks!" Then he lowered his head and growled at the gang of otters whose leader he had just sent swimming. "I think you all need a new leader . . . unless you want to hear me sing again? I've got enough song in me for each and every one of you."

The otters were bruised and banged from the coyote's first song and had no desire to hear another. One by one, they brushed themselves off, put their busted glasses back on their faces, and one by one, they opened their paws and lowered their heads to the coyote.

"We surrender," they said.

"What's your name?" one of the otters—a burly brute named Chuffing Chaz—looked up to ask, then lowered his snout back down toward the dirt.

"My name doesn't matter," the coyote told them. "You

can call me Coyote. And I welcome the Thunder River Rompers to my band."

"Band?" Chuffing Chaz asked.

"Oh yes," said Coyote, panting with glee. "You're my band. And together we'll make beautiful music."

The otters smirked, because they now knew what the coyote meant by *music*, and this time, they'd get to help him with the *singing*.

"Now." Coyote cleared his throat and picked his guitar up from the mud. "Who can tell me which way it is to a place called Ankle Snap Alley? That's where we've got a concert to perform."

Chapter Two

PALS OF THE PAW

IT'S not right to be awake so early," Eeni grumbled. Her tiny pink nose sniffed the chilly air, while her tiny pink paws scrambled along the pavement to keep up with Kit. The dry leaves crackled under her toes, snapping with the season's first frost.

Kit had to slow down for Eeni because just one of his raccoon steps was about six steps for a rat of her size. He looked over at his small friend, whose complaining, he had learned, was part of her waking-up routine.

Some creatures did jumping jacks, some stretched or groomed themselves, while others took a moment to give thanks to their ancestors, to the ground, and to the sky.

Eeni, however, could not fully wake up until she had complained about something for at least two hundred steps across Ankle Snap Alley. She was a street-smart, runaway albino rat who was slick enough to pick a kangaroo's pocket, but she was *not* a rat who suffered in silence.

If she was going to wake up early, she was going to whine about it.

"The sun's barely started to set!" she declared. "It's too bright out! It's too cold! The hedgehogs are getting ready to hibernate! Why don't rats hibernate? Or raccoons? We should hibernate! We should *all* hibernate."

"Looks like some folks are starting early," Kit observed.

Across the way, Brevort the skunk lay sprawled on the ground, snoring and drooling onto the rock he was using as a pillow. His drool had frozen into a long icicle on his furry face. His quick breaths made misty clouds in the air in front him.

Kit and Eeni crossed the broken concrete to the side of the Dancing Squirrel Theater. They clambered over the old tires and broken bicycles that littered the alley, charged through whitewashed heaps of trash and freezing weeds that prickled and tickled their tummies, and they stood in front of the skunk. He lay on the ground just outside the door of a place where no self-respecting animal ever set claw or paw. It was called Larkanon's, and luckily for the stray dog who owned it, there weren't a lot of self-respecting animals in Ankle Snap Alley. He did a brisk business in cheese ale and moldy snack crackers.

The sleeping skunk had on a dirty pair of striped pants that matched the stripe down his back. He snored louder than a bear, and his tongue lolled out of his mouth. His pockets lolled out of his pants the same way. Some citizen of Ankle Snap Alley had emptied the sleeping skunk's pockets of every last seed and nut he had.

"Wake up, Brother Brevort." Kit nudged the skunk with a paw, using his other to hold his nose from the skunk's pickle-and-graveyard stench. The skunk groaned.

"The Bagman's coming!" Eeni shouted, and Brevort sat bolt upright.

"Where? Where is he?" the skunk shouted. His tail shot up, ready to spray his stinky spray.

Eeni laughed, and Brevort frowned. "That's a lousy trick," he grumbled. "Telling a sleeping fellow the Bagman's coming."

"It woke you up, didn't it?" Eeni said.

She knew it wasn't nice. Every animal in Ankle Snap Alley was afraid of the Bagman. He was the Person who came to empty the ankle-snapping traps when animals got caught in them. When a fella went into the Bagman's bag and went away, he never came back. Some animal folk wouldn't even joke about the Bagman.

But not Eeni. There was nothing off-limits to her sense of humor.

Brevort rubbed his head, only noticing then that he had a single acorn clutched in his paw. He stared at it like a snake studying a shoe.

"Time to go home," Eeni told him. "You've been robbed, but they left you an acorn. Use it to buy yourself breakfast."

"Or eat it *for* breakfast," Kit suggested.

"Oh." The skunk looked down at his pockets, not seeming the least bit surprised that they'd been picked bare. "It was kind of them to leave me this acorn."

On the trees above the alley there weren't many acorns left. Even now, so early in the evening, the squirrels were busy above, bringing the last ones down to deposit in the bank.

The skunk stood, brushed himself off, and tipped his hat to the children, although he was not wearing a hat. "See you at the First Frost Festival," he said.

"See you," Kit and Eeni replied. The skunk stumbled his wild way back into the dark door of Larkanon's and disappeared.

"How many times has he had his pockets picked?" Kit wondered.

"I dunno," Eeni said. "I stopped doing it to him when I

was just a little ratlet. No sport in robbing that fellow. You almost feel bad for him."

"Almost," said Kit. "But folks make sure he survives the winter."

"Howl to snap," Eeni said. She held up her little pink paw to Kit's big black one.

"Howl to snap," he agreed. These were the words of Ankle Snap Alley, and saying them told everyone that you came from there and not some cozy field or forest out under the Big Sky. "Howl to snap" meant that even though you came into the world with a howl, and most creatures from Ankle Snap Alley went out again with the snap of a trap, you knew it was what you did in between that howl and that snap that made you who you were.

Kit had lived in Ankle Snap Alley for the whole leaf-changing season, ever since he'd lost his parents to a pack of hunting dogs, and he knew that all the animals who didn't live here thought the alley was just a nest of no-good dirty-rotten garbage-scrounging liars and crooks.

In fact, the alley *was* a nest of no-good dirty-rotten garbage-scrounging liars and crooks, but it was *his* nest of no-good dirty-rotten garbage-scrounging liars and crooks. Sure, they'd steal from a fella, but they'd always leave an acorn in his paw after they took ten from his pockets. In Ankle Snap Alley, folks looked out for one another, even when they didn't get along. There were folks in Ankle Snap Alley who cared about Kit, and folks Kit cared about.

In short, it was home. From howl to snap.

"Evening, Kit!" Kit's uncle Rik called out to them from across the alley. When Kit had lost his parents, it was his uncle Rik who had taken him in, Uncle Rik who had invited Eeni into their home when she had nowhere else to go either, and Uncle Rik who had enrolled them both in school for the coming winter.

Rik was a fuzzled old raccoon, prone to excitement over obscure bits of ancient history, more likely to trade his last seeds for an old book than a hot meal, but he was kind and generous, and in an all-too-wild world, a kind and generous raccoon was the best thing you could have on your side. Kit wouldn't mind at all if he grew up to be like his uncle.

Except for the big book collection. Who needed so many books?

Uncle Rik waved them over in front of Possum Ansel's Sweet & Best-Tasting Baking Company. Already, a motley crew of bleary-eyed animals were lining up for their sunset breakfast at the popular café.

There were three squirrels Kit recognized from the Dancing Squirrel Theater, two frogs from the Reptile Bank and Trust going over long scrolls of bark covered from end to end in writing, a young church mouse with a satchel full of pamphlets to hand out, a chipmunk in a tattered overcoat, a twitchy weasel with a briefcase filled to bursting, a company of moles in hard hats, a news finch in his press visor arguing with a loud starling about last night's rabbit boxing match, and a sullen-looking rabbit boxer with a black eye and swollen ear. At the front of the line, stood a pigeon named Blue Neck Ned, who had a way of cutting to the front of any line in the alley.

Uncle Rik ignored all the creatures waiting and thrust a piping-hot chew pie apiece into Kit's and Eeni's paws.

"Ansel made them specially for you for the first day of school," Uncle Rik told them. "Hazelnut crust stuffed with banana peel, fish bones, blue cheese, and candied worms! Eat up!"

Kit's mouth watered at the thought. "Are those fried rose petals on top?" Kit asked. Uncle Rik nodded. Possum Ansel was a genius in the bakery.

"Why should those kids get special pies?" Blue Neck Ned cooed. "I been waitin' here since the sun was up!" He pecked at the doorframe angrily. "Open up and give me *my* breakfast!"

The door swung open, and a big badger glared down at the pigeon, his paws crossed over the apron he wore. If Possum Ansel was a genius at baking treats, his partner, Otis the badger, was a genius at breaking beaks.

"Cut the noise!" Otis roared.

Ned gulped. "I just wanted to know why these two kids got served before everyone else? It ain't fair—"

"Fair?" Otis leaned down. He pointed a paw at Kit. "Don't you know who this is? He's the raccoon who saved the alley from the Flealess a few moons back! We'd all be dead and gone if it weren't for him!"

Kit smiled, feeling a rather proud and heroic.

"Hrmpf," Ned grunted. "What's he done for me lately?"

Otis shook his head and shut the door in Ned's face.

Uncle Rik ushered the kids away from the grumpy pigeon, who knew very well who Kit was and what he had done for the alley.

The furred and feathered citizens of Ankle Snap Alley had strange memories, Kit figured. They were always quick to forget a kindness, but they remembered every grief they'd ever come to. It'd be a better world if it worked the other way around.

But Ankle Snap Alley was not a better world.

"Well, Kit, you ready for the first day of school?" Uncle Rik asked him when they'd gotten back to the front of the Gnarly Oak Apartments.

"I guess." Kit shrugged. He'd never been to school before, so he didn't know how he could possibly be ready. How could you know if you were ready for the unknown?

"I think this whole school thing is a bad idea," Eeni

interjected. "I don't know how you talked me into going back."

"School is where you learn what you'll need to know to make your way in the wild world," Uncle Rik said.

"Do you think the First Animals made *their* kids go to school?" Eeni waved her pie around and spoke with a mouthful of crumbs. "Can you imagine it? The Great Mother Rat sending her little ones off to sit still and listen to some cheese-breath teacher? Ha! We should be out pulling off a heist and picking fights with the Flealess in their houses! Going to school? School's for the fishes! Are we not wild? Are we not free?"

"It's the First Frost Festival tonight," Uncle Rik said. "Winter's coming cold and fast, and we'll all need our wits about us. School's the best place to build up your wits, after all."

"I do fine on my own," Eeni said.

"No one does fine on their own," Uncle Rik replied. "We need each other. Just look at the First Frost Festival! It's the only time you can get every creature in this alley to cooperate on *anything*, and it's the only thing that lets us all survive the winter. You think some unschooled weasel came up with the idea for it? No! It was a creature with an education!"

"What do you think, Kit?" Eeni asked, trying get her pal on her side.

He shrugged. "I've never been to a First Frost Festival," he said. "So I can't say what I think about it."

"Oh, you'll love it, Kit," Uncle Rik explained. "A great tradition! There's a variety show and speeches, and fresh fried grubs, and everyone in the alley is there to deposit their winter supplies in the bank, and . . . well, you'll see it all tonight. It's a day of firsts for you! I almost wish I could go back twenty-five seasons and relive my *first* First Frost Festival. Oh, what a time! In school, I studied the habits of People and their Flealess house pets during the coldest months. While we celebrate winter by coming together, they curl up in their houses and pull apart. They use their clothing for warmth, rather than their fur. You see, People don't notice our clothing at all . . . think they're the only ones with fashion sense, so in winter, they dress their pets up in all sorts of poorly tailored outfits. I believe they learned the technique from Brutus, the Duke of Dogs, seven hundred seasons ago. Brutus had a porcupine for a tailor, you see, and all the animal folk went to him for their suits. Their hats, at the time, were made by a famous goose, if you believe it, the last of the bird haberdashers, who had a shop in what is now the—"

"Pardon me, Uncle Rik," Eeni interrupted him. "We do *love* your *long* history lessons about *fascinating* hats, but we really should be getting to school."

"I thought you weren't eager to get to school." Uncle Rik raised a bushy eyebrow at her.

"Well," said Eeni. "Like it or not, if we don't go now, we'll miss our ride."

She pointed up, and Kit's jaw dropped down in amazement as a berry-black cloud of bats swirled and whirled against the orange-and-red sky. The cloud rose and stretched, then swirled down straight for Ankle Snap Alley.

"Paws up, Kit!" Uncle Rik patted him on the back. "Time to fly!"

Kit gulped. Maybe Eeni was right and school *wasn't* such a good idea . . . not if you had to fly to get there!

Chapter Three

NIGHTFLIGHT INCORPORATED

SO, Eeni," Kit said to her as he watched the bats swooping in. "I've never, like, actually traveled by bat before."

"I figured," she said.

"I'm a little nervous."

The rat flashed him an insouciant grin—*insouciant* being one of her favorite words. It means carefree, easygoing, and unconcerned.

He couldn't even say the word *insouciant* without his teeth tripping over his tongue.

"In-soo-si-ant," he tried under his breath, where Eeni couldn't hear him practicing.

Kit was hardly feeling insouciant at all.

"Don't worry your snout off about flying," Eeni told him. "The bats have been taking kids to school for as long as older folk have been making kids go to school, and they hardly ever drop a student on the way."

"*Hardly* ever?" Kit gulped.

"Best keep your hat on tight." She stood on her tippy toes to smash Kit's hat down over his ears, just as the bats swooped in. "First time's the toughest."

A labor of moles dove for cover, the brood of chickens shielded themselves with their wings, and more than one frog hopped back into their doorway as if their lives depended on it. Almost every citizen of Ankle Snap Alley—scaled, furred, and feathered alike—got out of the way, except for the youngsters ready to go to school.

Kit watched a squirrel his own age stand on his back paws and raise his front paws over his head like he wanted to slap palms with the passing bats. Instead, a group of bats broke from the cloud and grabbed him by the wrists, hoisting him up off the ground, while a few more dove beneath him, flapping their wings under his feet and raising him up into the twilight sky.

Three mole siblings put their paws up and were whisked away in the same fashion, and so were a group of church mice in their matching robes, a young ferret who helped out the rooster at the barber shop, a baby-faced frog in his shiny winter coat, and a pack of gray rats with matching bows on their tails.

As he watched them leave the ground, Kit couldn't help but think that none of them were meant to fly.

One of the gray rats winked at Eeni as she passed overhead. Eeni stuck out her tongue.

"Old friends of yours?" Kit wondered.

"*Blech*," Eeni sneered. "I'd never be friends with *respectable* rats like the Liney sisters." If there was one thing Eeni disliked, it was a rat who considered herself respectable.

Kit suspected that it was the Liney sisters who chose not to be friends with a street rat like Eeni, but he was too polite to say it. Eeni was a proud rat, and a friend didn't chew holes in another friend's pride just because he could.

"Before you go, I wanted to give you this." Uncle Rik grabbed Kit by the paw and placed a small wooden token into it. Kit looked down at the disk in his black paw. It'd been made from a tulip tree, the kind that grew out in the Big Sky, where he came from. The wood was pale brown with delicate pink lines striped through it. It was old and roughly carved and had a symbol etched into it. The symbol showed a mouse's paw inscribed in a rat's paw, inscribed in a squirrel's, inscribed in a cat's, inscribed in a raccoon's, inscribed in a fox's, then a wolf's, and outward and outward, each claw and paw inscribed inside a larger one, all of them set inside the massive paw of a great bear.

"All of One Paw," Uncle Rik said. "The motto of your new school."

Kit wrinkled his brow.

"This belonged to your mother," Uncle Rik explained.

"Mom?" Kit looked up at his uncle, who had a gleam in his eye, a tear that he wouldn't allow to escape.

"I know she'd have wanted you to have it on your first night," Uncle Rik said. "She'd be very proud of you."

Kit studied the token, imagined his mother holding it in her paws, his mother giving it to him on his first night of school, if she were still alive. He sighed and tucked it into the inside band of his hat. "Thanks, Uncle Rik," he said.

"Of course, Kit," Uncle Rik said, and gave him a big raccoon hug. Then he backed away toward the door to his apartment in the Gnarly Oak. He nodded toward the cloud of bats swooping down. "Your turn! Stick with Eeni and she'll show you what to do!"

"Keep your paws up high!" Eeni ordered Kit, raising her paws over her head.

"Am I the biggest animal they're picking up?" Kit tried not to let his nerves give a quiver to his voice. He stood next to Eeni and raised his paws up.

"I guess you are," Eeni told him. "But don't worry. I've

seen the bats carry a full-grown deer without so much as slowing down."

"You saw that?"

"Well, I heard about it."

"From who?"

"You mean 'from whom'?" Eeni corrected him. "And I heard it from Silas, the porcupine who owns the tattoo parlor."

"And *he* saw it?" Kit asked.

"Well, no," Eeni said. "He heard about it from Rocks, who owns Larkanon's, who heard about it from Grumpkin, who used to own the Paw and Pawn shop, who heard about it from one of the Blacktail brothers . . . who . . . oh yeah . . . I guess the Blacktails aren't the most reliable raccoons."

"Reliable?" Kit gasped. "Those two raccoons would lie to the rain to sell it a rainbow!"

"I guess you better hang on extra tight, then, because here we go!"

Eeni raised her paws, and the cloud of bats stretched down to grab her. Kit barely got his own up in time. Eeni left the ground with a cry of "weeeeeee!" just as Kit felt the first tiny bat claw wrap around his wrist.

Another grabbed his elbow and another his pelt and another and another. More fluttered below him until all he could see were the flapping leathery wings and grayish fur of the bats all around him. With a stomach-turning lurch he was in the air. He'd dropped his breakfast pie, but saw it suddenly floating beside him, held up by one of the bats.

That bat—like all the bats—wore a small handkerchief with the company logo on it:

NIGHTFLIGHT
INCORPORATED
A Winged Carrier Company

"First time going to school?" the bat with the pie asked him.

Kit did his best to nod. He was too winded to speak. He could feel himself rising higher and higher, carried by dozens of tiny bat claws. "My name's Declan. Been with NightFlight since the first season I could fly. I seen it all up here, and then some. Best advice I can give a first-timer is this: Don't look down."

That was the worst possible advice to give a first-timer.

No matter the shape of your claws or the sound of your song, if you're a creature with breath and brains, when someone tells you "don't look down," you will always, in every circumstance, immediately do the opposite.

Kit looked down.

He really wished he hadn't.

Chapter Four

RACCOON IN THE MOON

BELOW his dangling paws, Kit saw Ankle Snap Alley dropping away. Possum Ansel and Otis the badger popped their heads from the bakery and waved up at him. Enrique Gallo, the rooster next door, flapped a wing at Kit before opening his barbershop, and Uncle Rik waved.

Lizards and frogs from the bank rushed to and from getting ready for the First Frost Festival; cats and mice, rats and weasels, hares and hens, darted this way and that, but they all glanced up at the cloud of bats carrying the students away. They got smaller and smaller the higher Kit rose.

Kit could see all of Ankle Snap Alley below him. There was the van where the mob of Rabid Rascals lived. Even now, the Blacktail brothers, twin raccoons of ill repute, were setting up their crooked gambling games for the night.

"*You may have luck, you may have plenty . . .*" Their voices faded as Kit rose.

There was the Dumpster market, where the scavengers made their deals, and there were the People's houses, their lights snapping on for the evening. Their spoiled house pets, the Flealess, stared up from the gleaming windows and shouted curses at the cloud of bats, curses their People could never understand.

"Lousy louse-riddled rodents!"

"Garbage-guzzling gutter goons!"

"Jerks!"

The last one wasn't creative, but the miniature greyhound who barked it at Kit made up for his lack of creativity with volume. Kit was amazed the loud bark didn't break the People's windows.

The world of Animal Folk and the world of People sat side by side, but neither took much notice of the other, and neither bothered much to understand the other's ways. Back in the time when the moon was new, when

People and animals shared the world as equals, they spoke one another's languages and knew one another's stories, but that was so long ago, it made as much difference as a fish's feet.

Kit didn't give the People much thought. Ever since he'd chased the Flealess from Ankle Snap Alley, he didn't give their house pets much thought either. They could bark and they could bite, but they'd never stop him from living his life.

He was happy in his alley.

But from high above, he saw how much, much more there was in the wide world. The view was enough to knock the skin off a salamander.

Kit rose above the top of the Gnarly Oak Apartments and waved at the news finches perched in its high branches. He rose above the rooftops of the houses, and he kept rising. The scurrying citizens of Ankle Snap Alley shrank to the size of ants, their stores and homes no bigger than anthills.

The train tracks beside Ankle Snap Alley vanished into an underground tunnel. The streets all around his alley had their own alleys behind them, although none looked quite so crowded with creatures as his own. He saw the tidy rows of rabbit hutches and chicken coops, shops with neat signs and well-tended burrows of raccoon and fox and stoat and mouse. He saw the lavish nests a flock of rich parrots had built for spending their summers in the city. Burly geese movers were packing the parrots' things for their flight south.

Ankle Snap Alley looked a poor sight indeed beside such wonderful neighborhoods.

He saw the big metal Rumblers that the People rode around in as they streaked along the concrete streets. They had white lights on their front ends and red lights on their rears, and People sat inside, staring forward. People couldn't see in the dark, so they made false light wherever they went.

Soon, Kit saw the People's massive towers with so many twinkling lights in their windows it was like they wanted to outshine the stars. These were the buildings that cut the sky into slivers, which was why all the animal folk called this the city of the Slivered Sky.

Kit's nose worked the high air. Through the stink of the bats he could smell that feathery musk of pigeons in flight and the tangy blood breath of hawks who'd flown this path in daylight. There were scents of steel and smoke, the crisp snap of cold air, even the dying leaf and grass smells carried on the wind from distant forests and meadows. The wind was a map written across his nose.

He breathed deep and smiled. How could he be afraid of heights when the world was full of such wonders?

"Hey, boyo, you gonna eat this pie?" the bat just above him asked.

Kit shook his head, and Declan nibbled the pie as they flew.

"How you like flying?" the bat asked.

"It's amazing," said Kit, looking down past his back paws at the rooftops of the giant city. Lights blinked and flashed and buzzed below.

"Guess so," said the bat. "But, you know, we got a tradition for first-timers like you."

"You do?"

"Yeah," said the bat. He smirked. "Probably smart you ain't eatin' this pie."

With that, the bat let out a sharp shriek and the other bats answered it. Kit swore he could make out the sound of laughter in the chorus of shrieks. One of the laughs, he thought, sounded an awful lot like Eeni's.

Before he could ask what the shrieking and laughing was about, Declan glided down beside Kit and whispered in his ear, "Try not to barf."

Suddenly, the cloud of bats wheeled wildly, turning in a sharp arc up toward the moon, then dove down so fast his stomach lurched. His legs kicked out, and his whole body swung sideways. He felt the tiny claws of the bats release his fur.

"AHHH!" he yelled. Nothing held him up, and he flapped his paws uselessly, his claws scrambling like they could catch hold of the stars.

They couldn't.

He fell.

His head tumbled forward, and his legs pointed at the moon. The buildings below shot up like jagged thorns on the rosebush of the world.

And then he was flying again.

Kit glanced over his shoulder and saw four bats, two per leg, flapping madly to hold him up. Before he could utter a word of thanks, the bats heaved him one way, then the other, then back again, swinging him like a leaf in a windstorm. As he arched upward, they let him go, tossing him into the cloud, where another swarm grabbed him, spun him, and threw him over their heads upside down.

"AHHHHH!" he added as the bats cheered.

"Come on, Kit, enjoy it!" he heard Eeni yell over the cheering bats. "They won't let you fall, I promise. Howl to snap!"

Kit found his voice as he dangled again in the claws of about eight bats. "It's the snap I'm worried about," he said. "My neck snapping when I hit the ground, mainly."

"Oh, we all go out with a snap sometime," Eeni yelled, laughing. "You might as well howl while you can."

"Easy for you to say," Kit told her.

He didn't hear Eeni's answer, because the bats had tossed him again. This time he did an accidental midair cartwheel, and he worried he might not be able to take Declan's advice about not barfing.

"I think this one wants to do some tricks!" the bat who caught him yelled.

"Woo-hoo!" the rest in the cloud cheered.

"No, that's okay," said Kit. "I really don't."

"That's what they all say," the bat replied.

"But I mean it!" said Kit.

"So did they!" The bats holding him laughed, then dove with Kit dangling under them.

They got going so fast Kit's lips pulled back from his teeth, but instead of screaming, he laughed.

He was flying and it was . . . fun!

The bats tossed Kit up to another set, and Kit opened his paws to catch theirs, using the force of the throw to spin himself upside down and let another group catch him by the back paws. That group swung him up over their heads, and he did a somersault.

"You could be in the Hopping Hare's Circus!" Eeni cheered.

"Woo-hoo!" Kit howled with glee.

In midair, falling past her from one set of bats to another, he reached up and tipped his hat to her.

"Nice tricks!" Declan said, flying once more at Kit's side. "Before you go I want to tell you about my performance tonight. I hope you'll be there!" He used his back claw to reach into a small pouch he wore around his waist and pulled out a piece of bark with an advertisement on it.

Dingbat Revue: The Comedy of Declan!
One Night Only, Live at the First Frost Festival

"So, you're a comedian?" Kit cocked his head.

"All bats are comedians. This flying transport thing is just our night job," said Declan. "I'm waiting for my big break in show business. I'm tired of performing at dirty saloons like Larkanon's."

"I bet you are," said Kit.

"Hey, you know what *kind* of a saloon Larkanon is?" The bat smirked. The other bats carrying Kit giggled.

"What kind of a saloon is it?" Kit asked.

"It's a . . ." Declan paused and grinned. *"A real dive!"*

All the bats holding Kit burst out in screeching laughs.

"Get it?" said Declan. "A *dive*? Like a really bad place . . . which they also sometimes call a . . ."

The only thing worse than a bad joke, Kit realized, was having a bad joke explained to you, so he decided to finish Declan's sentence for him. "I get it. A dive."

"You heard the lad!" Declan whooped. "He said 'dive'!"

And that was the real joke. Because at his command

the bats holding Kit dove straight for the concrete city below.

Just before slamming into the clear glass of a huge tower, they turned, so close Kit's claws scraped the windows. He stared briefly at his own reflection racing by, at a shocked Person on the other side of the glass, and then they turned along another street, dove again, and weaved through a maze of Rumblers that honked and screeched.

They flew through a tunnel and then up a wide avenue. Then turned sharply over the rooftop of a building and circled over a large round symbol made from smooth stones of all different colors. It was the same symbol on his mother's token, the paws inscribed within paws. It took up most of the rooftop, each paw outlined in different shining stones, all of them set inside a perfect circle of green stones the color of a summer leaf.

The bats set Kit down right in the center of it, directly in front of a flame-red fox. The fox wore a black felt hat and a purple jacket with long-trailing coattails. On his jacket he'd fastened a shining pin, emblazoned with the same symbol on which Kit stood.

Kit touched the tips of the claws of his front paws together to form an A, the symbol of greeting among his kind, but the fox just stared at him. Of course, the A was only a symbol for raccoons—after Azban, the First

Raccoon. Foxes had their own ancestors. Kit changed his paws into the crooked claw salute of the foxes, which the fox then returned.

"I am Mr. Timinson, your teacher," the fox said. "And you must be the famous Kit. Welcome to the academy."

Chapter Five

SHARP EYES

WHAT are we doing here, Boss?" Chuffing Chaz asked the coyote as he and the Thunder River Rompers gathered beneath a large pole beside the dark tunnel that led into the city. The otters were nervous. They didn't know what gang controlled this turf or what strange plans their new boss had for them now. They had never been so far from their river.

"Before we go to Ankle Snap Alley, we'll need a few friends with sharp eyes and sharper beaks," Coyote told them.

"You mean—?" Chuffing Chaz gulped and looked

straight up, two bright yellow moons reflecting off the lenses of his glasses.

The moons blinked. Two more appeared, then two more after that.

These weren't moons at all, but the wide eyes of three owls, staring down from their nest atop the high pole.

"Whhhooo goes below?" one of the owls hooted down.

"I've many names," Coyote called up. "In the Howling Lands, I'm known by my voice on the night wind. In the city wilds, I am a flash of gray against the red sunset. I am Hunger and I am Want and I am Power."

"You are a terrible poet." One of the owls left her nest and swooped down to land in front of the coyote and his gang. The other two owls watched from above. "And there is only one creature whhho makes such grand pronouncements in such terrible poetry. You are Coyote."

The coyote bowed. "In the flesh."

"Whhhat brings you to us?" the owl asked.

"My friends and I are on our way to a performance of sorts," the coyote explained. "And we are looking for friends like you to join us."

"Join you?" the owl said. "The Mercenary Sisters of Cement Row do not join gangs like yours. Wheee are hhhhunters for hhhhire."

"And I would like to hire you to hunt for me," Coyote said.

"Our fees are more than a lone coyote can scavenge in a year," the owl said.

"We are on our way to Ankle Snap Alley," the coyote told the owl. "Do you know the place?"

The owl raised her eyebrow, but said nothing.

"I assume by your silence that you do," Coyote said. "I have business to attend to, and it would make my business go far more smoothly if you and your sisters were watching over the affair. In exchange, I offer you a treat rarer than any owl has ever eaten."

The coyote glanced up and saw the other two owls swivel their heads toward each other and then back to him. He had their attention, of that he was sure.

"Have you ever heard of the Rat King?" he asked. "A hundred rats with their tails tangled together, moving as one, speaking as one, but feeding with a hundred mouths and seeing with two hundred eyes?"

"You mean the sage of Ankle Snap Alley?" the owl said. "Wheee knowww them."

Coyote scratched behind his ears, then leaned in close to whisper to the owl in front of him, knowing that her sisters could certainly hear him no matter how quietly he spoke. "How would you like to hunt the Rat King?"

The coyote didn't wait for the owl's answer. He turned and loped away, his gang of otters following him into the tunnel.

"See you in Ankle Snap Alley!" he called back to the owls. He knew they'd be there when he needed them. If there was one thing those three sisters couldn't resist, it was the chance to eat the most famous nest of rats the wide world had ever known.

And without their Rat King to turn to, Ankle Snap Alley would be easier to knock over than a dandelion in a hurricane.

Chapter Six

THE CLAW WITHIN THE PAW

THEY say you're clever as the First Raccoon but as kind as a church mouse," Mr. Timinson said to Kit, who stood in front of him in the center of the large paw-print symbol on the rooftop. "Is that true?"

Kit glanced around for Eeni, or any of the other students who had arrived before him, but he saw no one else on the roof except his teacher.

"I'm nice to those who are nice to me," he answered the fox.

"*Nice?* Hmmm . . ." The fox scratched behind his ear. "Nice and kind are not the same thing."

"They're not?" Kit was confused.

"*Nice* is how you want folks to see you," the fox explained, ignoring Kit's darting eyes. "*Kind* is who you are when no one's looking. I imagined someone from Ankle Snap Alley would know that. So which are you, *nice* or *kind*?"

"I'm . . ." Kit thought a moment. "I guess I try to be both."

The fox stared at him a long time with his bright yellow eyes. Then he broke into a wide grin and laughed. "Spoken like a true raccoon. I do hope you are as clever as they say, because at this academy your cleverness will be tested. We were founded by the last members of the Moonlight Brigade and we strive to live up to their example."

Kit frowned. He'd heard of the Moonlight Brigade before, but only in stories.

When the People built the first fires and left the animals in the darkness, the First Tricksters—Azban the Raccoon, Brother Rabbit, Elder Crow, Mother Rat, and Reynard the Great Fox—swore to remind the People that some wilds would never be tamed. They created the Moonlight Brigade to steal into People's homes, smash their traps, and howl at their heels. They created the Moonlight Brigade to protect every wild thing beneath the sky.

The only problem was, the Moonlight Brigade didn't exist anymore.

"Uh . . . sir?" Kit scratched under his hat. "The Moonlight Brigade isn't real."

"Not *real*? Have you not heard the story of the Rabbit Who Robbed the Farmer's Garden? The Crow Who Stole the Hunter's Fire? The Raccoon Who Won the Night Away?"

"I know the stories," said Kit. "But that's all they are. Just stories."

"Ha-ha!" the fox laughed. "*Just* stories, you say, as if stories mean nothing? Stories are the stuff that sticks the world together. Stories are the mud from which we're all made. The power to imagine stories is the power to remake the world as we dream it. That is what the Moonlight Brigade was. They were the Claw Within the Paw, the snapping jaws that kept the wilds free."

"They did?"

"Of course! Like Azban, the First Raccoon! Or Reynard, the Great Fox!" Mr. Timinson waved his paws in the air excitedly. "They dreamed of a world where animal folk did not fear the People, where our wild world prospered no matter how they hounded us. Let them keep their Flealess house pets with their endless cans of neatly packaged house-pet food. We hunt and scrounge and pilfer and pillage because we are free and our freedom lets us make the world as wild as we want it to be. In these dangerous times, when the wilds are ever shrinking, we must learn to defend ourselves! That is why the Moonlight Brigade existed, and that is why you are at this academy!"

"It is?" Kit asked with a smile. He liked the sound of that. It sounded grand and heroic, the kind of heroic that not even Blue Neck Ned could argue with. His chest puffed with pride.

"I meant 'you' in the plural sense." The fox snapped his pride in half. "Your generation. There are other teachers on other rooftops with other students, all learning the proud traditions of the Moonlight Brigade."

"Oh," said Kit, disappointed that his teacher didn't already think Kit was a great protector of the wilds. Didn't he know what Kit had already done? Didn't he know Kit had faced down a Flealess army and won? All he had to do was ask around. Kit was already a hero! Instead of offering this protest, however, he simply asked: "Aren't we a little young for all that, saving the wild world and stuff?"

The fox shook his head. "My generation has failed to protect our wilds, so it must fall to yours. Besides, if I didn't believe the young had power to change the world, why would I be a teacher at all?"

Kit shrugged.

"Are you ready to be tested, Kit?" his teacher asked. "Are ready to learn?"

Kit took a deep breath and nodded. He really, really was. He suddenly imagined himself as part of the old stories, the heroic raccoon who lead the Moonlight Brigade. So what if it wasn't real? Not everything that mattered had to be real. If he could dream himself great and heroic, maybe then he would be, just like the Moonlight Brigade of old.

"So, where *are* my classmates?" he asked.

"They're hiding." The fox turned, his puffy red-and-white tail swishing across Kit's face, nearly knocking his hat off. "You have until the count of ten to hide yourself too."

"And then?"

"And then I *hunt* you." The fox glanced over his shoulder and flashed Kit a razor-toothed smile. "Your lessons begin right now. One . . . two . . . three . . ."

Chapter Seven

HIDE 'N' HUNT

AS the fox counted, Kit looked left, and he looked right. They wasted no time at this academy. They also had precious few places to hide.

There was big metal tower on the roof, but one glance told Kit the three rat sisters were hiding there already. He could see the reflection of the bows off the metal in the moonlight.

A ferret's tail poked from an empty pipe, and anyone with half a nose could smell the deep dirt odor of the moles crouched tight in the cracks between loose bricks. Fergus the frog had tried to camouflage himself against the lip of the roof, but his shiny jacket gave him away. None of the creatures was as good at hiding as they thought. He didn't see Eeni anywhere, of course. She was a street rat, and a street rat didn't live long in Ankle Snap Alley if she didn't know how to make herself invisible.

"Four . . . five . . . six . . . ," his teacher counted, his tail swishing back and forth to keep the rhythm, his eyes shut tight but his ears perked.

Kit ran toward a big spinning metal fan, blades whirling and twirling, spitting hot air out from the building below. Steam billowed from behind it, clouding the blades in white. That wouldn't work. He ran the other way, toward a door that led inside the building. Locked, and he didn't have the time to pick the lock with his claws.

"Seven . . . eight . . ."

Kit ran to the edge of the building. He peered down.

A dizzying drop, the slick glass-and-metal walls offering little to catch on to if he fell. Down below, cruising across the thin ribbons of pavement, Rumblers rolled, white lights shining in front of them, red lights glowing behind. It was hypnotic to watch.

"Nine . . ."

Kit threw himself over the edge, hanging by his front paws, dangling over the side of the building. He wasn't the only one who'd had the idea to dangle. A squirrel named Dax hung right beside him, gripping the roof by a single paw. The other was extended to Kit.

"Hey, how you doing?" the squirrel asked, cool and casual. Squirrels had absolutely no fear of heights.

Kit kept both his front paws on the ledge.

"I'm good," he answered, wishing his voice hadn't come out squeaking like a starling's.

"You look nervous," Dax said. "You nervous?"

Kit nodded.

The squirrel twisted his body around, still dangling by just one paw. "Don't be nervous. Not like there's a wind." Just then, a freezing gust of wind ruffled their fur. "Well, be a little nervous—"

"TEN!" Mr. Timinson announced from above. "Now I'm coming to find you. It's a Hide 'n' Hunt. Whoever I find answers a question."

They heard the fox's claws crunch on the gravel of the roof.

"You all saw our seal when you arrived. This is the symbol of our school, and it is the symbol of the Moon-light Brigade, as it has been since the moon was new and the stars grew on trees."

They heard a yelp and a whoosh as the fox pulled the ferret from his hiding spot in the pipe.

"What does it mean?" Mr. Timinson asked.

"It means All of One Paw," the ferret said.

"Yes!" the fox told him. "Very good. And what does *that* mean? You!" There was a yelp as he hoisted a church mouse named Matteo from his hiding place. "All of One Paw?"

Kit peeked up from his hiding spot to watch. As the little mouse stood next to the ferret, the fox kept searching, putting the frog, the Liney sisters, and two more church mice in line beside him.

"It means we're all the same," the mouse answered. "No matter how big or small, how furry or, uh"—he glanced at the frog—"not furry . . . we're the same."

"The same? No matter how small?" The fox smiled. "A very mouse-like answer, thank you." Then he spoke so loud that his breath knocked the hoods off all the church mice. "But you could not be more wrong!"

He turned and looked right at Kit, who dropped down again as fast as he could.

"Nice going, Kit," Dax the squirrel said. "He saw us for sure."

Kit listened, his keen ears hearing the fox make his slow way to the edge. Closer and closer he drew to Kit's hiding place over the side, when suddenly, there was a sneeze. A rat-sized sneeze.

The fox stopped. His paws crunched the other way.

Kit peered up again just in time to see Eeni slide herself off the spinning metal fan to emerge, staggering and dizzy from the mist. "I had just about enough of hiding," she announced, and Kit swore she winked at him. "Anyway, I know the answer," she added.

"Very well," Mr. Timinson sat in front of her. "What does 'All of One Paw' mean?"

"That's the symbol on the roof," she said.

The teacher nodded.

"And on your pin?" Eeni added.

The fox nodded again. Eeni seemed like she was stalling for time.

"You want *me* to explain the symbol on *your pin* to you?"

"Yes, I do," said the fox.

Eeni sighed right into the teacher's face, then picked something out of her teeth with her tail. She was . . . what was that word? *In-soo-si-ant. Insouciant.* Eeni was, like always, unflappably *insouciant*.

"Can I look closer at it?"

The fox reached up to remove the pin from his coat, only to find it wasn't there anymore. He looked down at his jacket, and when he looked up again, Eeni was twirling the pin, perfectly balanced on the tip of her claw. The metal hummed as it spun.

The students in line gasped. No one had seen her paws move near Mr. Timinson's coat, but she'd swiped it right off him. She was the best pickpocket in Ankle Snap Alley, but Kit never imagined she would have the nerve to steal from their teacher.

"Never mind, I got it," she said. She made a great show of looking the pin over, while her teacher stared at her.

"All of One Paw means," Eeni said, "that our differences, like all the different paws in that pretty little pin, are what make us special. All our differences make the world what it is. We're not supposed to be the same. We're supposed to be the best version of ourselves we can be. For example, I'm supposed to be the sneakiest." She flipped the pin around in her paw, making it vanish and reappear again in the other paw. Then she flicked it in the air back to Mr. Timinson.

Everyone waited to see what the fox would do. Kit was surprised that instead of getting angry, the fox smiled. He wasn't like any creature Kit had ever met before. What should have made him mad made him smile.

"I was told you were a quick one, and I see I was told correctly," the fox said. "But you are not entirely correct either." Eeni frowned as the fox turned back toward where Kit and Dax were hiding as he fastened the pin back on. "You two can come out now! You've been found."

"Drat," Dax said, and bounded up to the roof with a single jump. Kit had to strain and scrambled his claws against the side until he threw himself onto the roof flat on his belly. No one ever said raccoons were graceful.

"Dax?" the teacher asked. "What are the black vines that run between the People's buildings?"

"They're . . . uh . . ." The squirrel clearly had no idea.

"You squirrels run across them every day, and you don't know?" Mr. Timinson shook his head. "They carry messages for the People. Signals and sounds and barks. They carry electric flame. What happens when you chew through them?"

"Uh . . ."

"I am amazed you have lived this long." The fox shook his head again and pointed Dax to join the line of students. "We have a lot to learn if you're to be all the squirrel you can be. Now, Kit?"

Kit stepped forward.

"Recite for me the five qualities of Azban, the First Raccoon," he asked Kit.

"Quick of Paw, Slick of Tongue, Brave of Heart, Afraid of None, and . . . uh . . ."

The fox cocked his head, waiting patiently. Kit's mind went blank. He searched his memory. What was the fifth quality of Azban? He couldn't remember! He could feel his teacher's patience running out. He was failing. How could he ever live up to the stories of the Moonlight Brigade if he couldn't even answer a simple question about his own ancestor? His lip started to quiver; shame boiled any thoughts he had left in his brain.

And then he saw Eeni. Her tail was bent around her head pointing down at herself. What was she trying to tell him? Why would his friend be pointing at herself while he was trying to answer his teacher's question?

His *friend*. That was it! She was giving him a hint!

"A Friend to All in Need of One!" Kit declared. "That's the fifth quality of Azban. Quick of Paw and Slick of Tongue, Brave of Heart, Afraid of None, and A Friend to All in Need of One."

"Very good," said Mr. Timinson. "Even if you had some help." He glanced at Eeni with a smirk, then spoke to the entire line of students. "None of you, it seems, yet understand what All of One Paw actually means. It is not just our school's motto; it was the motto of the Moonlight Brigade itself. It was their highest ideal!

"Therefore, your first assignment to complete by to-morrow night is this: You must speak to a kind of creature you never have before and tell the class one thing you've learned about them. Be bold. I am not interested in hear-ing what your grandfather mole has to say about the old days. I want you to expand your world. If it's easy, you're doing it wrong. Extra credit if it's a hunting creature with whom you speak. Of course, try not to get eaten in the process. It looks bad if too many of my students get eaten during the first assignment, understood?"

"Yes, Mr. Timinson," the class responded.

"Good," he said. "Now, I believe your bats are arriving to take you home. I hope you all enjoy the First Frost Festival."

"Thank you, sir," the Liney sisters responded sweetly.

The fox nodded and trotted off toward the empty metal tower where they had been hiding.

"Wait!" Kit called out. "*That's it?* That's all school is? Just asking a bunch of questions and not telling us the answers?"

"Shh," Eeni groaned. "Don't make it *longer*. I thought it would never end. All those questions! Who cares about cans of food and Flealess history? Live in the now! That's what I say."

"But we were barely here at all," Kit said. "And we still don't know what All of One Paw means!"

The fox trotted back over to Kit. "What did you think school would be, Kit?" he asked. "Sitting around listening to the mice read aloud while I correct their spelling?"

"No," Kit said, realizing he had no idea what school was actually supposed to be like.

"Learning is what you do out in the wild world," Mr. Timinson said. "It is my job to give you the tools to do it. That won't happen up here on a rooftop. Enjoy your festival, do your assignment, and I'll see you tomorrow night. Maybe by then you will have figured out what All of One Paw means on your own."

The fox strolled away again, and Eeni crossed her paws, staring at Kit. "You!" she said. "You almost got us *more* school!"

"I just thought we'd get a chance to show Mr. Timinson how clever we are or—"

"I swear, Kit, you are the strangest raccoon I've ever known." Eeni shook her head. "If you weren't my best friend I'd think you were crazier than a groundhog in a sandbox."

"Is that a saying? A groundhog in a sandbox?"

"It is now," said Eeni. "I just said it."

Kit laughed. He liked the sayings Eeni made up, even when they made no sense.

"Why do you want to impress the teacher so badly?" she asked.

"Did you hear all that stuff he said about the Moonlight Brigade?" Kit said. "It sounds awesome, don't you think? The Claw Within the Paw! I want to live up to *that*! I want to *be that*!"

"You want to be in an imaginary ancient brigade that drove the Flealess and their People crazy?" Eeni asked.

Kit nodded eagerly. He really, really, really did.

Eeni chuckled and gave him a friendly flick of her tail. "Let's get to the First Frost Festival. Even the Moonlight Brigade enjoyed some fried grubs and a show, I bet."

"You think I have what it takes?" Kit asked. "You think I'm clever enough to be like they were?"

"Well, you're the cleverest raccoon friend I've got," Eeni said, sticking her paws in the air for the bats.

"But I'm the *only* raccoon friend you've got," Kit replied, putting up his own paws.

Eeni winked at him as the bats swept in and hoisted them away.

Kit had no idea what to expect from the First Frost Festival, but thanks to Coyote and his gang it would be a show that no one in Ankle Snap Alley would soon forget.

Chapter Eight

DINGBATS

THE First Frost Festival was one of the oldest and most important events in all of Ankle Snap Alley. Every animal who called that rusted, rutted, crooked, and cratered alleyway their home came out on this one night, just as the winter's first frost began to settle.

The Dancing Squirrels performed their tail-waggle jig, the NightFlight bats performed their comedy act, and guest bands came on and off for musical entertainment.

None of the performances, however, was the reason all the animals came to the festival. Ankle Snap Alley was not known for its love of the arts.

The animals came because the First Frost Festival was the night when the alley made sure it would survive the long, cold winter to come.

"You see, Kit," Uncle Rik explained as they took their place in the crowd, facing the makeshift stage the moles had built. "The show is just to give folks something to do to keep them from brawling while the real business goes on at the Festival. The *bankers'* business."

Kit glanced to the side of the stage at the Reptile Bank and Trust. It was an unassuming entrance, just a broken block of heavy white stone veined with thin blue lines into which the reptiles had carved their sign: a picture of a snake coiled around an acorn. Below the large stone sat the bankers' vault. It was kept under the guard of a brightly colored frog rumored to be so poisonous that his own children couldn't hug him without risking certain death. He sat on an upturned spool beside the narrow entrance, his big eyes twisting this way and that, watching every movement of the assembling crowd.

"The real business," Uncle Rik continued, "is the genius of the festival. In the old times, after Azban, the First Raccoon, passed into the endless moonlight, and the Moonlight Brigade vanished with him, there was chaos in the alley. When the cold season came, the hoarders hoarded and the hunters hunted, and every creature plotted the downfall of every other. The animals spent all winter trying to rob and cheat one another out of their stored seeds and nuts. Hibernating was out of the question, lest someone else rob you as you slept and left you to starve. Being awake didn't help much either. The strong preyed on the weak, and the weak tried to outwit the strong. Paw versus Claw. Our society was in disarray. Winter became such a dangerous time that most folks packed up and left. Ankle Snap Alley would hardly have survived, but for the bankers and their plan. They decided that on the first frost all the creatures in the alley would deposit their winter stores in the bank—all their seeds and all their nuts and anything else of any value.

"It would all be carefully cataloged and controlled by the reptiles, who have a perfect reputation for cold-blooded security. Even the Rabid Rascals gang put their wealth into the bank for winter, and said that anyone who didn't do likewise would get a claw in the eye."

Kit shuddered. He didn't like the Rabid Rascals one bit. Everyone in Ankle Snap Alley was a bit of a crook, but the Rabid Rascals were the worst of them. They'd been as cruel to Kit as the Flealess had, but he still had to live alongside the Rascals. They were in charge of the alley, after all. And they were his neighbors.

"Oh, they're not all bad," said Uncle Rik. "They're the ones who decided to make this into a party."

"Folks around Ankle Snap Alley will put up with a lot of crooks as long as they throw a good party," added Eeni.

"When the air begins to bite and the white frost falls upon us," Uncle Rik continued, "we gather with our neighbor—gangsters and church mice alike—and we celebrate the season gone by, while we store our seeds for safekeeping. Thanks to this festival, we can withdraw them from the bank all through the snowy winter months, without a care for scrounging and scurrying about in the snow. This way, we *all* survive."

"But isn't it dangerous?" Kit wondered, glancing around at all his neighbors. They all had sacks and satchels, bags and boxes stuffed with all their worldly wealth. "There are more thieves here than there are leaves left on the trees. What if someone gets an idea to, I don't know"—he glanced at Eeni—"pick a pocket?"

Uncle Rik patted him on the back and laughed. "Fear not, my nephew! The Rabid Rascals provide security. Anyone caught stealing at the First Frost Festival is dealt with . . . severely."

Kit saw the gang members weaving through the crowd. Stray dogs and grumpy pigeons, mean-eyed ferrets, and even a feral cat or two. The Old Boss Turtle, ruler of the Rabid Rascals, watched over them from the roof of his van. Beside him, the gecko who was in charge of the bank sat with his long ledgers and read over the deposits. It was quite a sight, the gangster and the banker together, all the reptilian power in Ankle Snap Alley in one place.

Meanwhile, in the crowd, the whole neighborhood was abuzz with activity. Possum Ansel and Otis the badger had their winter supplies in two large crates. They were entertaining a traveling woodchuck from a northern forest who had a large quantity of sweet tree sap to sell. Ansel couldn't wait to bake it into a sap-and-smoked-sardine pudding.

A newt in a blue suit stood nearby, ready to document the deal.

Glass bottles filled with lightning bugs lit the performers onstage, although no one was paying them much attention. The chickens were gossiping, the gangsters were prowling, and the news finches were arguing with one another about the night's news. Declan, the NightFlight bat, hung upside down on a rolling perch below a circle of lightning bugs in the center of the stage. A sign in front of him said

Dingbat Revue: The Upside-Down Comedy of Declan!

"Here he goes!" Eeni said, passing Kit a small bag filled with deep-fried grubs soaked in zucchini butter. They were crunchy and salty and still warm. He wondered whether she'd bought them from the refreshment gopher or swiped them when he wasn't looking.

He decided not to ask.

Declan told his jokes as loudly as he could over the sound of talking and arguing in the audience.

"What do you call a bat with no sonar?" Declan shouted, paused for dramatic effect, then answered his own question. "*Lost!*"

The bat slapped his tiny thighs.

No one laughed.

He didn't give up.

"I once met a bat with no sonar. He was flying in circles, and I said, hey, friend, where do you want to go? And he told me, I want to go to the bathroom. I said, but you've got no sonar, how are you *guano* get there?"

Declan looked out at the crowd. Not so much as chuckle.

"Get it?" Declan tried. "*Guano.* I'm a bat . . . our poop's called *guano*? Get it? How are you *guano* get there?"

Brevort the skunk burped, which was, in truth, much funnier than Declan's joke.

"What do you call a bat who never leaves his cave?" Declan asked, loosening the handkerchief around his neck. "*Rock*-turnal."

Crickets actually chirped.

Then the audience started throwing them at him.

"Hey, I love crickets!" Declan shouted. "Looks like I get a free meal! And I thought I was the only *dingbat* here!"

"Boo!" a few members of the audience shouted. "Boo!"

A pygmy goat in a floppy bow tie ambled onto the stage and used his head to roll Declan's perch off.

"Y'all wouldn't know comedy if it bit you on the neck!" he shouted as he was rolled away.

Once Declan was gone, the masters of ceremonies stepped under the ring of lights.

Shane and Flynn Blacktail, raccoon twins of ill repute, had taken up the job of hosting the First Frost Festival together after the squirrel who usually did the honor had an unfortunate accident. He'd stepped on one of the People's animal traps that still littered Ankle Snap Alley. He'd actually snapped his ankle.

It was an odd thing that that trap had been in the squirrel's living room at the time.

Everyone was pretty sure the Blacktail brothers had arranged that accident to give themselves a chance to perform. They were the sort of raccoons who wanted to be stars of the stage and were willing to break a leg to make it happen, but only if it was someone else's leg.

"Hey, brother?" Flynn said to Shane, while facing the audience and striking a pose. "A question for you!"

"Yes, brother," Shane said to Flynn, also looking out over the audience and striking a different pose. They'd both dressed in their finest vests and wore colorful cravats around their necks.

"Did you know that bats were nocturnal?" Flynn asked.

"Of course I knew that, brother," said Shane. "Just like raccoons, they're awake at night."

"*Not* just like raccoons," said Flynn. "Because tonight, that bat put me to sleep!"

To the side of the stage, which was called "the wings" because that's where birds hung out, Blue Neck cooed once, laughing at the brothers' joke. Ned never heard a mean joke he didn't like.

"Friends of the fur!" Shane exclaimed to the audience. "We've a new act tonight, making their Ankle Snap Alley debut! A musical act. Pals o' me paw and my brothers in beak, even you cold-blooded lizards counting out the seeds, for the first time at our First Frost Festival, let's hear a warm squawk and a cluck and a hoot and a holler for . . ."

Flynn pulled a note out of his pocket to read the name written there: "Coyote and the Thunder River Rompers!"

Chapter Nine

EVERYONE'S
A CRITIC

NO one squawked or clucked or hooted or hollered when Flynn introduced the coyote. They were too busy counting out their seeds and nuts, waiting in line to deposit them, looking warily at one another and watching the Rabid Rascals roam among them.

On top of the stone slab of the bank, Old Boss Turtle was whispering instructions to his porcupine henchman.

The church mice in their white robes stood around a large rolling cart, on which they'd placed their chests and sacks of seeds and nuts, bits of hard cheese, and their most treasured possession, their printing press. The church mice were the scribes of Ankle Snap Alley, proud guardians of all its written words. A few of the younger mice weaved their way through the crowd, giving out pamphlets proclaiming the mouse philosophy.

Possum Ansel and Otis the badger were doing their best to keep their visiting woodchuck from noticing the pickpockets, gamblers, and claw-slipping creeps that lurked in the crowd, all while keeping a wary watch on the Rabid Rascals too.

Every merchant in the alley paid the Rascals "protection seeds," which basically meant turning over some of the seeds and nuts they earned honestly so that the gang didn't tear their shops to shreds. The Rascals also kept anyone else from tearing their shops to shreds. They were as close to the law as existed in Ankle Snap Alley, but if they didn't like the shape of your snout or the glint in your eye one night, they could pound you into the mud for sneezing and no one would stop them.

They were an unlikely bunch to protect the festival, but Ankle Snap Alley was an unlikely place. Kit got to thinking that if the Moonlight Brigade were still around, they wouldn't need the Rabid Rascals to protect them. They'd be safe from anything.

As Kit pondered the heroic past, Shane and Flynn stepped offstage with flourishing bows and a fearsome gray-and-brown coyote strolled underneath the lightning bugs.

He had a tin-can guitar around his neck, and a trio of otters in dark glasses behind him. One otter had a comb flute hanging around his neck, another a set of drums made from a can, a bucket, and a bottle. A third had an old jug to blow a breathy bass note on.

"My friends of the fur and of the feather," the coyote said, his voice resounding and rich, as if a western wind could talk. "And, yes, my scaly friends too." He bowed gracefully to the frogs and lizards at the bank. "It is a pleasure to be here to make music for you tonight. I've traveled all the way from the Howling Lands to entertain you with a song I've sung in the palaces of hawks and in the grand caverns of the bear council. I've sung at hummingbird communes and at crow carnivals! I've sung to the great and to the small alike, those rich of seeds as well as those whose only wealth is the love in their hearts, and now I'm delighted to sing to you at your First Frost Festival."

"You believe this guy?" Eeni rolled her eyes. "He's cheesier than a church mouse on alms day."

Kit cleared his throat, but didn't agree with Eeni. He thought the coyote was mesmerizing. This was a creature Kit would like to talk to. This was a creature who'd earn him extra credit. The other animals had begun to take notice of Coyote too.

As the big animal stalked the stage, shifting from light to shadow, his fur rippled over the powerful muscles of his shoulders and legs. It was as if the air itself had parted to let him pass.

Possum Ansel and Otis the badger stopped chatting with the woodchuck, while Enrique Gallo cocked his head side to the side, trying to find the best view with his tiny rooster eyes. The bright bird beside him fluffed her feathers and tried to get his attention back with no success. She gave up and watched Coyote too.

Even the Old Boss Turtle stopped looking over his lists of who had put their seeds in the bank for winter and who still needed to, and stuck his neck from his shell to watch, and the coyote hadn't even begun to sing yet.

It seemed only Eeni was immune to his charms. She was a rat who was not easily impressed.

It didn't help that coyotes had been known to eat a prodigious number of rats, a point she tried to whisper to Kit, who shushed her when Coyote raised the guitar in his paws and prepared to make his music.

"*Prodigious* means 'remarkable in size,'" Eeni explained.

"Shh," Kit interrupted her. "I've never seen a coyote before. I want to hear his song."

The coyote strummed his guitar once.

The twang of brand-new strings over the tin can produced a chord that rattled and coughed, not so much a musical note as the sound of the city itself. Then he howled, piercing, raw, and completely uncivilized.

"Owwwwwooooooooooo!"

This was the sound of the world outside the city, the sound of the Big Sky and the Howling Lands.

The audience hung in the silence that followed that howl, and the coyote cast his gaze around with a grin that showed all his sharp teeth.

"Hit it, boys! Ah one and ah two and ah one two three four . . ."

With that, his band sparked to life. The comb flute player played his comb flute, and the jug blower blew his blowing jug. The drummer drummed and Coyote strummed, and every one of them began to hum.

And it was a disaster.

Kit had heard geese with stomach flu make more beautiful music. He'd heard moles scratching through concrete that made sweeter sounds. And when the coyote finally sang, his voice was like a duck choking on a pinecone.

"I've had cheese ale with the Duke of Dogs.
Ow ow owooo!

And I've lost at cards to a one-legged frog.
Ow ow owooo!
But shave my hide and clip my claws,
I broke no laws, with these two paws.
Ow ow owooo! Ow ow owooo!"

The otters burst into a chaotic jam session, none of them following the same tune. While they played, Coyote danced around the stage, jerking his limbs this way and that, throwing his head back and howling, then standing on his back paws and hopping. No one had ever seen an animal dance like that before, and for good reason. It looked more like a severe case of Foaming Mouth Fever than a dance.

"*Ow ow owwooooo!*" Coyote howled.

"I don't think any of them know how to play their instruments," Kit said.

"I don't think they're really a band," Eeni said.

Kit's fur prickled. Some animals could sense when a storm was rolling in or could tell when a ship at sea was about to sink. Kit, like any orphaned animal who had lived long enough to grow his whiskers, had a knack for sensing trouble before it bit.

"Kit, look." Eeni swiveled her head around the crowd. More otters in dark glasses had slipped from the shadows and stood at the back of the crowd, surrounding it on all sides. They weren't carrying instruments in their paws. They were carrying weapons: clubs and saw blades, branches and slingshots.

"We gotta get out of here," Eeni told him.

"Uncle Rik?" Kit tugged at his uncle's fur.

"Shh," Uncle Rik said, brushing him off. "I am watching this performance. Do you think this is some kind of traditional coyote dancing or does he have a medical condition?"

"But, Uncle Rik, there's—" Kit was interrupted as the audience started to boo the coyote.

"Boo! Boo! Boo!" the whole audience chanted together, even the banking lizards.

"Don't quit your night job!" Blue Neck Ned cooed.

Coyote raised his paws in the air, and the band stopped playing. He sat down on his haunches and gave the audience a sad-eyed hangdog look.

"You don't like my song?" he whimpered. "I guess I should've known the folks of Ankle Snap Alley were too sophisticated for my simple country singing."

"You call that singing?" a starling yelled. "You wouldn't know singing if the great Maestra Nightingale sang for you herself!"

The Blacktail brothers stepped out onto the stage to try to calm the crowd and to introduce the next act, but

Coyote didn't move away. When the goat came to shoo him off, he let out a long sigh and took the tin guitar from his shoulders and held it by the neck.

"Don't be too hard on yourself," Shane Blacktail told the coyote, patting him on the back.

"Yeah . . . *let us do it for you!*" Flynn Blacktail laughed. "You make music as well as a chicken flies."

"But, brother," said Shane, with false surprise, "chickens don't fly."

"And coyotes don't make music!" Flynn delivered the punch line like it was a real punch.

Coyote frowned.

Kit felt his tail twitch. Nothing good was about to happen, of that he was quite sure.

"Uncle Rik," he whispered. "We gotta get out of here."

"I guess you boys are right," Coyote told the audience. "I'm no musician, and my fellas here ain't either. But I came to Ankle Snap Alley for two reasons: to sing my song and to rob you blind. And I guess I'm all done singing."

Uncle Rik glanced back as the otters surrounded the crowd, and his whiskers twitched. "You are absolutely right," he told Kit, and took him by one paw and Eeni by the other to lead them from the growing danger.

But it was too late.

The next sounds anybody heard were Shane and Flynn

Blacktail's shrieks as Coyote knocked them headfirst off the stage with a mighty whack from his guitar.

CLANG! AEEEEEEE!!!

At that, the otters rushed into the crowd and began one of the oldest traditions of Ankle Snap Alley, older even than the First Frost Festival itself.

They started a brawl.

Chapter Ten

THE SONG OF TOOTH AND CLAW

OTTERS clubbed and clawed, pressing the creatures together to prevent their escape. Uncle Rik pulled Kit and Eeni along, making his way toward the tunnels below Ankle Snap Alley, when suddenly a large otter loomed before him.

"Where do you think you're going?" the otter growled. He raised a club and swung it straight for Rik.

Uncle Rik shoved Kit and Eeni out of the way. He let go of their claws so he could block. His tough paw met the club with a *THWACK,* and his strong black fingers wrapped around it.

He tugged at the otter's weapon, but the otter tugged back.

"Grrrr," the otter growled.

"Grrrrr," Uncle Rik growled back. "Get out of here, kids!"

"Eeni, I gotta help Uncle Rik," Kit said. "You should go."

"What kind of friend only sticks around for the fun stuff?" Eeni replied. "You know me better than that!"

He did. And he was glad to have her at his side as they rushed toward the big otter.

"The Farmer's Wife?" Kit suggested.

"The Farmer's Wife," Eeni agreed quickly.

There was an old story from the days of the Moonlight Brigade about a farmer's wife who cut the tails off three blind mice. It was a story People told their children and animal folk told theirs, but each took different lessons from it.

Kit tapped the otter on the shoulder, and the otter reached around with his free paw to try to catch Kit's tail. Before he had the chance, Eeni had slipped around and swiped the glasses off his face.

"Hey!" he roared, and lost the grip on his club, which

Uncle Rik yanked away from him. When the otter tried to grab at Eeni, Uncle Rik whacked him on the shins.

"Ow!" howled the otter, falling to the dirt.

Eeni held his glasses out in front of his nose, taunting him. "You want these back?"

"Gimme!" the otter bellowed. "I can't see!"

"First tell me, are you a hunter?" Eeni asked. The otter nodded.

"Eeni?" Kit wondered. "What are you doing?"

"My homework," she said. The otter tried to grab the glasses back, but Eeni's paws were too quick and she moved out of his reach. "Nuh-uh," she scolded the otter. "First tell me one thing I don't know about you otter folk."

"My name is Chuffing Chaz." The otter squinted up at her. "And I never forget an insult," he snarled.

"What a terrible way to live," Eeni told him. "I try never to remember an insult. But thanks for getting me extra credit on my assignment." She curtsied and tucked the glasses away into her pouch.

"Hey!" the otter yelled, but she and Kit and Uncle Rik had already moved away from him, trying to get out of the brawl.

The scene was crazier than an anthill under a dance hall.

Creatures scrambled over one another to escape the

kicks and punches of the otters. Birds who could fly took flight only to be grounded again by slick stones fired from the otters' slingshots.

Possum Ansel clung tightly to Otis. The badger had two otters in a headlock and was swinging them around like battering rams, clearing a path. Enrique Gallo swiped left and right with his razor-sharp talons, and the pack of stray dogs who guarded Old Boss Turtle had formed a circle around him, snarling and growling to make their own way out.

None of them made it.

Coyote's otters onstage fired lit matches from rubber-band bows right at the escaping animals' fur. The strays cowered and whimpered with their paws over their heads. Otis dropped the otters and threw himself on the ground, rolling this way and that to put out a fire on his forehead, while Ansel blew on the burning tip of his possum tail. The air reeked of singed fur and burning feathers.

Old Boss Turtle poked his head out of his shell long enough to yell, "A winter's worth of acorns for anyone who gets me out of here safely!"

Blue Neck Ned fluttered up to rescue him, but was knocked beak over tail backward by Coyote himself, wielding his guitar as a cudgel.

"I really do love this kind of music!" Coyote shouted

over the roar of the riot. "The song of tooth and claw! *Ow ow owoooo!*"

"It's a beautiful tune, Boss," another otter replied gleefully, just as he dropkicked the turtle's porcupine henchman straight into a mass of panicked news finches. The poor fellow, once feared by every creature in Ankle Snap Alley, now found himself on his back, his quills stuck upside down in a sack of seeds and nuts, his paws scrambling helplessly in the air.

The bankers from the Reptile Bank and Trust tried to get as many of the sacks of seeds into their vault as fast as they could, before all the fortunes of Ankle Snap Alley fell into Coyote's paws.

An otter hopped down in front of the stone entrance, knocked a gecko in a suit out of his way with one paw, and grabbed the colorful poisonous frog with the other.

Unfortunately for the bankers, and for all the rest of Ankle Snap Alley's citizens, the frog was not at all poisonous. He was a normal green frog who'd painted himself bright colors so he could double his salary from his banker bosses.

He pretended to faint before the otter had a chance to clobber him or the bankers had a chance to fire him.

"Enough!" Coyote howled so loud that the even the clouds seemed to pull back from the moon, shining brightly on him.

The fighting ceased, and all the animals of Ankle Snap Alley were left groaning and licking their wounds. "We could play this song until the sun comes up," Coyote explained, striding once more across the stage. "Or you could surrender every seed and nut you've got and spare yourselves more bruising."

The silence that answered him was even heavier than the silence that had followed Declan's comedy routine.

"Why don't I make this easier for you?" Coyote suggested. "Turtle!" he called. "You might as well stick your head out before my friends haul it out through the back of your shell."

The turtle stuck his head out, his deeply wrinkled face showing all its long seasons. He spoke slowly and quietly so that the coyote had to strain to listen.

"You have messed . . . with the wrong . . . turtle," the turtle said. "No one . . . pushes around . . . my . . . Rabid Rascals. We own . . . this . . . alley."

"Not anymore." The coyote shrugged. "Please order your goons to collect every seed and nut in the bankers' vault."

"Eat a tick sandwich," Old Boss Turtle snapped.

Coyote leaped in one terrifying bound down into the dirt in front of the turtle. He lowered his head and picked the old turtle up in his jaws and shook him mercilessly, rattling the reptile around inside his shell. Then he set the turtle down on his back and rested a massive paw across the unprotected belly of the gangster boss. Coyote pushed down with all his weight.

"How hard do you think I'd have to push to crack your shell?" Coyote asked.

The citizens of Ankle Snap Alley looked away and buried their faces in their paws so as not to see the brutal scene. They'd all suffered at the gangster's claws over the years, but this was too much to watch.

"Would you now instruct your gang to collect every last seed and nut in this alley for me?" Coyote asked.

Kit couldn't hear what the turtle said.

"Louder, please!" Coyote demanded.

"Do it," groaned the old gangster. "Collect the seeds!"

"You hear that?" the coyote howled. "Rascals! Get to work. You!" He pointed to Shane and Flynn Blacktail. "I'm putting you two in charge. Congratulations. You're the new leaders of the Rabid Rascals."

Through bloody snouts, the brothers grinned.

"If you hold out so much a single dried pokeberry from that bank vault, then my boys and I will sing you another song. Get it?"

"Howl to snap," they answered.

"Now have your gang collect my loot," he ordered them.

Shane and Flynn hopped to it with the enthusiasm of the newly powerful.

"Come on, boys, you heard the fellow," Flynn told the gang.

"He's not much of a singer, but you know the tune," said Shane. "Get to it."

The mix of mutts and birds and other surly creatures looked around questioningly, but one by one, they moved through the crowd, making merchants and dancers and gamblers of every size and shape turn over their winter seeds. They sent a scurry of squirrels into the bank vault below to haul out the seeds and nuts that had already been deposited.

When the raccoon brothers reached the merchants, Possum Ansel was defiant. "Why did we pay the Rascals for protection, if they couldn't protect us?" he demanded.

Shane and Flynn looked at their feet, stung by a brief pang of shame. The turtle groaned on the floor below. Even criminals such as these had taken pride in their work and were embarrassed to have been out-crimed by a tougher criminal.

"Just turn over the loot," Shane pleaded.

"The sooner you give it up, the sooner he'll be out of our fur," Flynn added.

Possum Ansel crossed his paws. The Blacktail brothers snarled, and Otis the badger jumped up to stand by his side. Coyote turned and delivered a single claw-jitsu kick to Otis's chest, knocking him into the waiting paws of two otters, who put him in a choke hold.

Possum Ansel passed out at the sight, in the time-honored tradition of possums everywhere.

"And we'll take your woodchuck's sap supply too," Coyote told Otis.

The badger frowned, but nodded.

"I can't hear you!"

"We will pay," Otis grunted.

"Good!" Coyote smiled.

A tiny voice shouted from the crowd. "A lot can happen between the howl that brings us into this world and the snap of the trap that takes us out." It was Martyn, leader of the church mice, in his bright white robes, surrounded by the other mice of his religious order. "Justice *will* come to bandits, even those who think they'll be strong forever."

"Ha-ha!" Coyote laughed. "You're talking about stories of the Moonlight Brigade, aren't you? Those stories are as stale as your breath. Besides, my stories are just as old as yours, mouse. And in *my* stories, Coyote always wins."

"You only know the stories you like to hear," Martyn replied. "We mice know them all, even the ones coyotes prefer to forget. The past is a wheel of cheese, and it rolls around and around. What was nibbled once will be nibbled once again, and justice comes to all eventually."

Coyote shrugged. "Right now, your winter seeds are what comes to me." He turned to a weasel in a shining coat who was trying not to be noticed as he stuffed all his seeds and nuts into his mouth at once with the idea that it was better to eat his fortune than to let it be taken from him.

Coyote lifted the sack away from him and passed it to a waiting otter. The weasel swallowed his last gulp of food.

One by one the creatures turned over the sacks and trunks and chests and bags, even the usually quarrelsome news finches, and when the entire alley had given over all they had to the coyote, he clapped his paws together and howled so loud that the hawks in their distant mansions in distant neighborhoods heard the sound and wondered what such a howl might mean, but hawks can't be bothered with the goings-on in the gritty alleyways of the city, and none would come to investigate.

All the animals watched sadly as their worldly wealth was turned over to the Thunder River Rompers.

"When bears battle, it's the grass that breaks," Eeni murmured to herself. She had a saying for every occasion, but Kit didn't like this one. He didn't want to be some broken blade of grass beneath the feet of bears. He wanted to be the hero who kept the bears away. He wanted to be like the Moonlight Brigade was, but what could one young raccoon do against a cruel coyote?

"The cold season's coming!" Uncle Rik stepped up to the coyote. Kit held his breath, seeing his uncle go snout to snout with such a ferocious animal. Uncle Rik ran a nervous hand over his fur, then puffed his chest proudly and made his argument. "Without our stores of seeds and nuts, we'll all starve."

A few other animals dared murmur their agreement.

"Your starvation is not my problem," said the coyote. He looked over the room and smiled. The animals' panting made hundreds of breathy clouds in the air. "Well, Rompers, we've done a good night's work. Let's be on our way. There's a whole city before us and much more music to make!"

"WAIT!" Kit shouted. He cleared his throat and yelled in his meanest voice, "What kind of broke-down bandit are you, Coyote?"

All eyes turned to look at him.

"What are you doing, Kit?" Eeni whispered.

"*My* homework," Kit whispered back. "I want that extra credit too."

Eeni grabbed his paw. "You aren't supposed to get eaten in the process."

Part II

FLIM-
FLAMMERY

Chapter Eleven

THE BAMBOOZLE

THERE have been many names for tricks since the moon first showed her friendship to thieves. They've been called lies and they've been called grifts and they've been called swindles and frauds and scams. They've also been called confidence games, gambits, flimflams, and pranks, but they're all the same thing: A trick is a trick, and the one who pulls it is a trickster.

And raccoons, of course, are great tricksters.

The greatest tricks of all are like stories, as grand as any epic tale bound in the pages of a book. A great trick has separate parts, like the beginning, middle, and end of a story. There are even characters in a trick, just like in a story, whether they know they're in a trick or not.

The first part, the beginning of a trick, is called the Bamboozle. The Bamboozle is the part where the one being tricked—the rube—gets lured in. This is where the plot is laid, the traps are set, and the biggest lies are told. The middle part of a trick is called the Sting. This is where the rube gives the trickster exactly what the trickster wants without knowing they've done it, and the third part—the final one—that's the toughest one of all. The third part is the Brush-Off, where the trickster gets rid of the rube, one way or another, and flutters away free as a butterfly.

All great tricksters, like all great storytellers, crafted these parts in their own ways. The Blacktail brothers did it with fast talk and sharp claws. Eeni did it with quick paws and sweet words. Kit didn't know exactly how he was supposed to do it, but he had only one chance to save Ankle Snap Alley from a winter of starvation.

If the coyote escaped with all their seeds and nuts, the Wild Ones would surely go hungry when the cold snows came. There wasn't enough tasty trash to keep them all alive for winter, and it would be like the old times, when the strong ate the weak and the weak choked the strong on their bones.

Ankle Snap Alley would fall to pieces if he didn't find

a way to stop this coyote. And maybe he could impress Mr. Timinson at the same time. He'd sure like to prove that he was as clever as Azban and twice as kind. *Was that too prideful?* he wondered.

Nah, he thought. *Raccoons don't have much in this world, just their cleverness and their pride.* He meant to do his best with both of them. He said a quick prayer to Azban, and then he let his great grift begin.

Time to bamboozle the coyote.

He had a plan.

"Did you hear me?" Kit repeated as loudly as he could. "I'm wondering what kind of timid tail-tucking thieves you and your gang are to come here and steal from us?"

"Kit, be quiet! Please let the adults handle this," Uncle Rik pleaded.

"What did you call us, little fellow?" The coyote whirled on Kit.

"Well, *first* I called you and your otters broke-down bandits—"

"We ain't broke-down!" Chuffing Chaz protested, looking in the wrong direction without his glasses. "We're the Thunder River Rompers! The baddest, brawling-est beasts this side of the sun!"

The other otters barked a chorus of agreement.

Kit cleared his throat. "After that, I wondered what

kind of timid tail-tucking thieves you are. I should have added snail-sniffing snot scavengers too, by the way."

If a crowd could gasp as one, the crowd trapped at the First Frost Festival did it at that moment. The gasp made Kit's whiskers wiggle.

He couldn't back down now. Great tricks were won or lost in the first precious moments of the Bamboozle. Just like telling a story, if you lost your audience's attention even for a second, you might never get it back.

"Now that I look at the loot you've taken," Kit continued. "I see you're just a bunch of seed-sucking muskrat moochers." He tried to act—what was Eeni's word?—*insouciant*. He played it as cool and carefree as he could. He hoped the gang didn't notice his tail quivering. He stood on top of it. "Anyone can rob an alley guarded by a gang as goofy as the Rabid Rascals. That doesn't make you tough. We got robbed twice last moon, didn't we?"

The animals of Ankle Snap Alley looked at Kit in confusion.

"*Didn't we?*" he repeated.

"Oh yeah," said Eeni. She couldn't know what mischief Kit was making, but she knew he needed help making it. Kit and his wits had never let her down before. "We got robbed three times, wasn't it?"

"Oh, right." Kit gave her a wink. "Three times. And the last time was by a group of voles."

"*Little* voles," Eeni agreed, even though all voles were little. "Cute ones. I don't even think they were a gang. I think they were a choir group."

"They did sing beautifully," agreed Kit. "Unlike some gangs I could think of . . ."

Coyote growled, which showed Kit that Coyote was still listening.

"So go ahead." Kit opened his paws. "Rob us of what little we have left, and word will go out that the Thunder River Rompers are just as bad a band of bandits as a chorus of voles."

Voles, it should be noted, were the least criminal of all the creatures who ever scurried beneath the moon. They were the cousins of mice, but smaller, gentler, and more timid. The worst crime a vole ever committed was eating the crumbs left over from the cookies they'd baked for their neighbors. And even then they remembered to send themselves a thank-you note.

"We eat voles for breakfast!" Chuffing Chaz bellowed, which caused two actual voles in the crowd to dive into their empty seed sacks.

The coyote shook his head at his own gang. "Don't get your tails all twisted. This little raccoon's words aren't worth much when I'm the one holding all his alley's winter stores."

"But what's a coyote like you want with a lot of seeds and nuts?" Kit asked. "I thought you were a hunter."

"Good point," Coyote snarled. "Would you rather I eat raccoon meat?"

"Raccoons are stringy," Kit squeaked before clearing his throat and speaking with more confidence. "You do not want to eat raccoon. What you want is your food served up nice and neat in cans like the Flealess get. A real bandit would want the Flealess food, not our paltry piles of winter seeds."

"Or the minuscule meat on our bones," Eeni added. The other animals in the alley agreed with her heartily. No one was eager to see the view from inside the coyote's jaws.

"Cans?" Coyote asked. He leaned forward, curious.

"Oh, never mind," said Kit. He reached into his pocket and pulled out his seed pouch. "You want all the seeds we've got, so don't forget mine. I was going to buy quills for school with it, but please, take it and show the wide world what kind of bandits you really are."

Chuffing Chaz groped forward and snatched the seed sack from Kit's paws. He stuffed it into his own satchel without looking. Coyote kept staring at Kit, sizing him up.

"Tell me more about this Flealess food," Coyote said. "In cans."

"You don't have cans of food out in the Howling Lands?" Kit asked.

Coyote kept eyeing him, but he didn't say yes and he didn't say no.

"Well," Kit explained, "the Flealess—that's People's house pets—they eat food from cans that their People put out for them. Fish and meat and grains and vegetables, all sorts of nice things that wild folk like us couldn't dream of. Sometimes we get their leftovers when they toss the empty cans in the trash."

"What good does a bunch of Flealess food do me?" asked Coyote. "It's in those houses, and I'm out here. No one breaks into People's houses and lives to tell about it after."

"Raccoons do," said Kit. "Rats too. Why last week my friend and I broke in to three People's houses just for fun."

Eeni nodded. "We had a party."

"I wore a party hat," Kit added.

"You lie," Coyote said. He turned to Shane and Flynn Blacktail. "He lying?"

Kit looked to the Blacktail brothers and held his breath. With his paws low, he made the symbol of the A with his fingers, the sign of Azban and of all raccoons. He hoped those two flea-bitten traitors would go along. If they didn't, he was as good as dog meat.

"He's lying," Flynn said.

"Kit didn't break into the People's houses last week," added Shane.

Kit's heart sank.

"It was *two* weeks ago," Shane continued.

"Last week was *our* turn to do it," said Flynn and flashed the A sign back at Kit. The brothers could smell which way the wind was blowing, and now it blew toward Kit.

"Oh, right," said Kit. "I forgot. We take turns. Howl to snap."

"So what?" the coyote told him. "Why should *I* care what *you* alley vermin do? I've got what I came for."

"But what if you could get you *more* than you came for?" said Kit. "What if I could get you double your weight in cans of Flealess food, straight from the People's houses?"

"*You?*" Coyote raised an eyebrow.

"It's a simple offer," said Kit. "Give us our seeds and nuts back, and I'll give you all the cans of Flealess food you can carry."

"You will?" The coyote cocked his head sideways.

"I will," Kit said. "Just give me two sunups' time, and I'll give you more food than you could ever steal from any neighborhood of Wild Ones in the whole city of the Slivered Sky."

"You wouldn't be trying to pull a little trick or me, would you?" Coyote asked. "A scam? A fraud? A bit of flimflammery? A *Bamboozle*?"

"Me?" Kit looked around the alley at his beaten and bruised neighbors, shivering in the morning chill. "I wouldn't know a Bamboozle from a bumblebee. I could never dream of trying to trick a coyote as wise and well traveled as yourself."

"I thought I was a snail-sniffing snot scavenger?" The coyote raised a bushy eyebrow.

"Well, that was before we got to know you." Eeni jumped into the conversation. "Now we see that you're shrewder than a shrew in shiny shoes, we'd be awfully glad to make this deal with you. It's a win for us and a win for you too."

"But we are, of course, at your mercy." Kit bowed.

The coyote snorted. "You *are* at my mercy . . . and I *will* take this deal."

Kit bit his cheeks to keep from grinning.

He'd bamboozled the coyote even though the coyote didn't think he could be bamboozled. As the First Raccoon once said, *A trick's well begun, when the Bamboozle's well done.*

It looked like Kit's trick was well begun indeed.

Chapter Twelve

DEALING AND STEALING

JUST as Kit was feeling good about himself, Coyote suggested a few "adjustments" to the deal.

"I will keep all the seeds and nuts I've taken until I have my cans two sunups from now," he told Kit. "You'll get it all back when you come through with your end of this bargain."

"Fair enough," said Kit.

"And I will take some additional *collateral* as well," the coyote told him. "To keep you honest."

"Coal-lat-er-all?" That was a word Kit didn't know and neither did Eeni.

"It means something I hold on to until our deal is done, something valuable to you that I get to keep if the deal should fail. Collateral is my insurance that you come through."

"But you already have all our seeds and nuts," Kit objected.

"I want something you value more," said Coyote. "Something truly irreplaceable." Coyote nodded at his otters. "Grab the turtle," he barked. An otter seized the Old Boss Turtle. Then Coyote smiled at Uncle Rik. "And this fellow here."

An otter to raised his club and knocked Uncle Rik out with one quick smack to the top of the old raccoon's head. Two other otters tossed him in a sack.

"Hey!" Kit cried out. He rushed forward, but Coyote pushed him back.

"If you ever want to see your uncle again, Kit," the coyote told him, "you'll get me those cans two sunups from now."

"Uncle Rik!" Kit shouted, but the shape in the sack didn't move at all. Kit started to feel sick. He'd been foolish to speak up. He'd thought he was only putting himself at risk by standing up to the thieving coyote, but now he'd put his uncle in danger too. He'd wanted to be the hero, but he hadn't thought about innocent bystanders. "How did you know he was my uncle?" Kit asked.

"Oh, Kit, you've become famous even out in the Howling Lands . . . the Hero of Ankle Snap Alley," Coyote said. "I came all the way here to see what you were made of. It's no accident I chose to rob Ankle Snap Alley. I wanted to meet you, the great hero of the Wild Ones, the little orphaned raccoon who foiled the Flealess." Coyote laughed. "Now that I see you, I have to laugh. A hero with a tear dripping down his cheek. Ha!"

Kit was stunned and angry. He wiped the tear from his cheek with his tail and snarled at Coyote.

"That's more like it," Coyote said. "Show some fight! Now let's see you save your alley again. And in case you get any ideas about rescuing your uncle before I get my cans of food, know that I have some friends with sharp eyes and sharper beaks who'll be keeping watch over you."

Coyote let out one high-pitched bark, and three shadows screeched over the alley. Then three horned owls, all of them in camouflage hunting cloaks and floppy camouflage hats, landed around the crowd, towering over the small creatures, their yellow eyes glowering.

The Mercenary Sisters of Cement Row had joined Coyote's gang.

"It was a pleasure robbing you all." Coyote bowed with a flourish. "I will see you in two sunups."

His gang hoisted the sack with Uncle Rik in it onto their cart with all the seeds and nuts and trash and treasure that had been held in the Reptile Bank and Trust. He barked at Shane and Flynn to push his cart. The raccoon brothers were in his gang now.

"Traitors!" Eeni shouted at them, but Kit put out his paw to stop her.

He stared at the two raccoons. "We always knew they were crooks," he told her. "Everyone from around here knows not to trust them."

"That's right," said Shane. "*Bees buzz and finches fly.*"

"*Raccoons cheat until the day we die,*" Flynn finished his brother's rhyme.

Kit growled and Flynn growled right back, but the Blacktail brothers left with the gang of otters and all the food the alley had.

"Hold on!" Chuffing Chaz plodded over to Eeni. "Gimme my glasses," he grunted at the empty air next to her, squinting.

"Why should I?" Eeni folded her arms.

"Because I'll club your brains into your tail if you don't!" the otter told her.

Kit rushed to his friend's defense, but she was already handing over the otter's glasses.

"I can't argue with your logic." Eeni sighed.

"And your seeds," the otter grumbled.

Eeni pulled out her seed pouch and dropped it in his paws. "Careful how you spend it."

Chaz put his glasses back on and put her pouch into his satchel next to Kit's. He huffed once, rejoined his gang, and vanished into the dawn.

The alley settled into a silent state of shock. They'd been robbed of everything they had, and their dangerous Rabid Rascals had totally failed to protect them. Now their hopes all rested on Kit's fuzzy head.

This was how the Moonlight Brigade must have felt in the old times, the whole weight of the wild resting on their snouts.

But if they could do it, then so could he! Kit would not let his alley down. He would not let his uncle down. He would save them all.

"Why'd you defend those Blacktail brothers?" Eeni asked him. "They hate you."

"They're our neighbors," said Kit. "They'll come through for us in the end."

"They've never come through for us before."

"Then I guess it's not the end," said Kit.

Eeni shook her head. "You didn't give that otter your real seed pouch, did you?" she asked.

"Nope," said Kit. "You?"

"Nope," said Eeni. "I gave him my snout surprise."

Both of them carried an extra seed pouch, a decoy

known among pickpockets as a snout surprise. It had a thin layer of seeds on top, but just below that was a brittle white wasps' nest. When the otters opened the pouches later and their big paws crushed the wasps' nest, they'd get a nasty surprise and a lot of angry stings.

When you lived in Ankle Snap Alley but weren't big enough or mean enough to fight, you needed a trick or two to keep the bullies away.

"Those otters are as dumb as moths at a bonfire," Eeni said. The sun had begun to fog the night sky with its first pink breath of morning. "So you bamboozled the coyote. What now?"

Every creature in the alley looked at him, frog to mole and finch to vole.

"Now?" Kit took a deep breath. "It's time for the Sting."

"How you think you're gonna do that?" Blue Neck Ned demanded.

"Indeed, it is not as if we have countless cans of fine Flealess food lying around the alley," Martyn the church mouse said as politely but sternly as he could.

"I'm gonna do just like I said," Kit told them all. "I'm gonna break into the People's houses. I'm gonna rob the Flealess, get my uncle back, and save our alley." He stood up tall and felt like the hero he was meant to be. "And I'll make that coyote wish he'd never come here."

Chapter Thirteen

OUTNUMBERED

"THAT was a crazy deal you made," Eeni told Kit, as all the other animals went scurrying to their burrows before the sun burned away the dark. "Please tell me you have a plan."

"I'm working on it," Kit told her. "But I'm going to need some advice."

"You're not seriously thinking about—?" Eeni stopped in her tracks and pressed herself against the wall of Possum Ansel's bakery.

"Yep," said Kit. "I'm gonna go see the Rat King."

"But we don't have an appointment," Eeni told him. "No one sees the Rat King without an appointment. In fact, other than you, no one has seen the Rat King in more moons than there are leaves on the trees."

"If I didn't know better," said Kit, "I'd think you were afraid."

"Me? Nah. I'm not afraid of anything."

Eeni tried to act casual, but her tail twitched. Kit knew she was scared of the Rat King. The Rat King was a creature made of a hundred rats tangled together. They spoke as one, acted as one, but saw with a hundred pairs of eyes and ate with hundred different mouths. They were the fortune-teller of Ankle Snap Alley, and they were also said to be quite insane.

That was not, however, why Eeni was afraid.

Eeni was afraid because one of those tangled rats was her mother.

Like all the first daughters in her family from the dawn of ratkind until Eeni broke the tradition by running away, her mother had joined the Rat King. She'd tangled herself and added her thoughts, her ideas, and her memories to it. From that long-ago night on, she was no longer Eeni's mother. She was just one part of the many-headed rat, the way one drop of water is one part of a pond. She was the Rat King, and she would never leave until her last breath left her.

Eeni's mother had, in a way, chosen the vows of the Rat King over her own daughter. She'd made Eeni an orphan.

Kit could understand Eeni's worries about seeing her mother again, but the Rat King was the wisest animal in all of Ankle Snap Alley, and if anyone could help with his scheme to rob the Fleales of their food, it would be Him. Or Her? Them. They were a Them.

"Let's go see 'em," Kit said, leading the way out of Ankle Snap Alley.

"Wait?" Eeni called after him. "Now? But the sun's coming up! It's time for bed!"

"We can sleep or we can survive," Kit said. "But right now, we don't have time to do both. I guess it's up to you, but *I'm* going to the Rat King to ask for help. Uncle Rik is counting on me."

Eeni gave a wistful look toward the door of the Gnarly Oak Apartments, and Kit could almost see her imagining her nice cozy bed. She sighed. "I'm right behind you, Kit, like always. Howl to snap."

"Howl to snap," he answered, and they scurried through the shrubs and darted across the big concrete road to the fence where the Rat King's owl bodyguard stood.

Except the owl who guarded the Rat King's lair wasn't in his usual perch.

He wasn't in any of his unusual perches either.

He was gone, and the fence had a big hole in it. Big enough for a coyote to crawl through with a gang of otters.

Their footprints traced a dreadful path in the dirt, leading straight to the open wall of the Rat King's home.

"Oh no," Eeni squeaked. Her fears forgotten, she raced ahead, and Kit had to run to catch up, scrambling over the rubble of crumbled wall that Eeni had scurried underneath.

He caught up to her at the edge of the empty pool where the Rat King lived. Worm-gray sunlight oozed through the broken windows and the air was heavy with silence. The last time Kit had been to see the Rat King, he had heard hundreds of claws clattering across the tiles and a hundred mouths chewing until a hundred voices spoke to him as one.

Now, nothing.

"Hello!" Eeni called out. "Anyone here? Hello?"

The wind didn't even bothering howling in response.

Eeni looked up at Kit, her eyes damp. "Where could the Rat King have gone?" she said. "They wouldn't just leave us, would they?"

Kit knew that when Eeni said *they* she really meant *she*.

She really meant her mother.

He rested his paw on his friend's back. He didn't have answers for her but could still offer the comfort of friendship. If her mom was really gone, then she'd become even more like Kit than she'd been before. An orphan twice over.

"You know, sometimes you have to shed your summer coat to grow in thicker fur for winter," he told her.

Eeni sniffled. "What?"

Little seeds of wisdom were really Eeni's thing, but he had to try to tell her *something* to make her feel better.

"Like, I mean, sometimes when you lose something important, you gain something else you need. Like when I lost my parents last season, I never thought I could survive, but I did, and because I did, I found Ankle Snap Alley and Uncle Rik . . . and *you*. My friend. If my life never changed, it never would have changed for the better either."

"That's real nice to say, Kit." Eeni wiped her eyes with her tail. Then she gave him a playful punch on the arm. "You're as sentimental as a skunk in a sewer."

If Eeni was making up nonsense sayings, Kit figured she was feeling better.

"I think we should look for clues where the Rat King's gone," Kit suggested. "A hundred-headed rat can't up and vanish into thin air without leaving some trace behind."

"Shh!" Eeni shushed him.

"What? I'm just saying—" Kit had thought she wasn't upset anymore, but maybe he'd been too quick to start hunting for clues while her feelings were still raw.

"I heard something!" Eeni whispered.

Kit's ears twitched. He couldn't hear anything unusual, but his nose worked the air. There was a smell he knew, something odd but familiar. Something he'd smelled on the breeze and in the trees and, most recently, at the First Frost Festival.

"Owls!" he and Eeni said at the same time, just as a screech sliced the silence and the great wide wings of three owls descended over them.

"*SCREEEEEEEEECH!*"

Kit dove to the left and Eeni dove to the right, and the owls' talons swiped at the empty air where they had stood an instant before.

When Kit popped back up to his paws, the Mercenary Sisters of Cement Row had landed around them, circling but keeping their wide eyes fixed. They closed the circle in, pushing Kit and Eeni back to back. The hunters blinked in sequence, one at a time, so that two of them always had their eyes open. There was no hope of escape.

"It's past your bedtime, little ones," one owl said.

"And long past ours too," another one added.

"We get grumpy when we're awake past sunlight," said the third. "Especially when we're hungry."

"Where's the Rat King?" Eeni demanded of them, turning this way and that, trying to keep her eyes on all three at the same time. They all knew that an owl could swallow a rat like Eeni without even chewing.

"Scurried off," one of them said.

"Seems they've got more sense than you two," another said.

"Rats know when it's time to flee a sinking ship," said the third.

"Ankle Snap Alley's not a ship," Kit objected. "And it's not sinking!"

"That was a metaphor," the first owl explained. "The ship stands for the alley, and we are the water dragging it down."

"And here comes the flood!" The owls rushed forward, sharp beaks snapping.

Kit rolled into a ball and threw himself forward. He knocked Eeni from their path and bowled through one of the sisters, but found his roll suddenly stopped with a painful yank on his tail. He sprawled on the hard bottom of the pool and looked over his shoulder. One of the owls had his black-and-white tail gripped tight in her talon. Another held Eeni up by the scruff of her neck, about to drop the squirming white rat into her mouth.

"What a tasty-looking morsel," the owl said. "Does a white rat taste the same as a gray, I wonder?"

"No, we're much more sour," Eeni replied. "And quite unhealthy. Wouldn't you rather have a delicious piece of lettuce or something?"

"Hush now, little one," the owl said. "It's just the way of the world. Owls eat and rats get eaten."

The owl let go of Eeni, and she fell toward the open beak.

"No!" Kit yelled. Eeni shut her eyes tight.

Then there was a hollow *oomph*, and Eeni landed face-first on the ground. The owl had been kicked onto her back against the other side of the empty pool and lay stunned as a swoosh of red fur leaped for the other two.

Mr. Timinson, their teacher, delivered a sharp punch to the belly of one of the owls. He ducked below the second, grabbed her talons, and swung her in a circle, tossing her onto her sister before she could even stand.

One of the sisters flew at him, talons up. He waited until the last instant, then flipped over her back and pinned her wings to her sides.

She fell and skidded across the rough cement. The fox hopped from her back, flipped her over, and clamped his jaws on her throat. He growled, and his meaning was clear.

The other two sisters froze in place.

"Fit's hime fur oo dooo gooo," he said.

"What?" said one sister.

"Don't talk with your mouth full," said the other.

"He says it's time for you to go," Eeni told them, brushing herself off. She jabbed an angry paw in their direction. "And don't you come back here threatening us again or we'll wallop you a second time!"

"*We?*" The owls smirked. "Your schoolteacher can't protect you forever."

"He doesn't need to," said Kit, who moved to stand beside Eeni. "I've got two nights to keep my end of the bargain with Coyote. Until then, you watch like he said, but you lay so much as a feather on anyone in Ankle Snap Alley, and I'll make sure the coyote knows you're the ones who cost him his cans of food."

"He'll destroy you all if you don't give him what you promised," the owl said.

"But he'll destroy you first," said Kit coldly. He needed to show these owls he wasn't backing down, even though, at that moment, standing in front of their terrible beaks and razor-sharp claws, all he wanted to do was back down and run home and hide under a blanket with a hot mug of spiced rose petal tea.

But heroes didn't hide.

Or drink rose petal tea.

The owls fluffed their feathers and bowed politely. "Please give us our sister back, and we'll be on our way."

The fox snarled but released the third owl from his grip. She gave an angry hoot, and the sisters flew through an open window and out into the bright morning.

"Well, students." Mr. Timinson turned and sat in

front of them. "I see you are making some progress in your homework."

Kit and Eeni stared at him, slack-jawed and dumb-struck.

"Kit, I hear you had an interesting conversation with a coyote," Mr. Timinson continued. "And, Eeni, you appear to have gotten to know an otter named Chuffing Chaz."

"Well . . . I . . . ," Eeni stammered.

"Rather bold choices by both of you, of course, for a first homework assignment, but I admire it," the fox continued.

"We would've been bird meat if you hadn't shown up to fight them off," Kit said, feeling less the hero and more the raccoon in need of rescue.

"We foxes have our vows too," Mr. Timinson said. "*To those who want wits, we provide them. For those who lack wits, we deride them, and when a friend is in need, we're beside them.*"

"But we aren't friends," Eeni said. "You're our teacher."

The fox cocked his head. "I was a friend to someone close to Kit and I promised her that I would look out for him if he ever came my way."

"Her? You mean—"

"I knew your mother," Mr. Timinson told Kit. "And she told me to look out for you. She hoped you'd be in my class. She knew you'd grow up to be something special, with the right guidance."

Kit reached into the inside band of his hat and pulled the wooden token out to look at it. His mother's token.

"She hoped, when the time came, you would be the kind of raccoon who could steal a star from the night, trick a dog from its tail, and outwit the Flealess and the coyote with a plan the rest of us couldn't possibly imagine," Mr. Timinson said. "Just like an ancient Moonlight Brigadier."

"She believed that about me?" Kit sniffled.

"She did," said Mr. Timinson. "Of course, all parents believe that about their young. It's the reason they don't eat them as soon as they're born."

"Oh," said Kit, frowning. "Do you believe it about me?"

Mr. Timinson stared back at him with gentle eyes, but he did not say yes. "What I believe doesn't matter," he said. "I am your teacher. It is up to *you* to become the raccoon you want to be."

"Oh," said Kit again, swallowing hard and studying the emblem on the coin some more. *All of One Paw.* Every paw had its own role to play. Was that what it meant? There were teachers and there were friends and there were hunters and thieves and there were tricksters. What role was Kit meant to play? He wanted to play the hero, but he always got other folk hurt when he tried.

"You *do* have a plan, don't you, Kit?" Mr. Timinson said.

"I really could've used the Rat King's advice," said Kit.

"I'm sure you could have," said Mr. Timinson. "But the Rat King knows when it's time to make themselves scarce, and you don't have time to wait for their return. Like the salamanders say, *You can't wish for a river when you're stuck in the muck. You gotta swim in the river you're in.*"

"My plan's not really a plan yet," said Kit. A plan for the second part of his trick, the Sting, had started to form in his mind, but there were a lot of missing pieces. Coyote knew the stories about Kit defeating the Flealess, so it was those stories that Kit would rely on to trick him. But he wasn't sure yet how to do it. "It's more like a daydream," he told the teacher. "I don't know how to make it happen yet."

"Well, you'll have some time to think about it tonight," said Mr. Timinson. "During our field trip. We're going to look for inspiration."

"We are?" Kit wondered. "Where do they keep inspiration?"

"At the carnival, of course," said Mr. Timinson. "If you've got any seeds left in your pockets, you'll want to bring them along. The carnival's a great teacher, but the crows don't give away its lessons for free."

Kit wasn't so sure a class trip to a carnival was the

best use of his time. His uncle was knocked out in a sack, and the alley was headed toward a winter of starvation. Every passing moment was a moment closer to Coyote's deadline.

"If a trickster can't find inspiration at a carnival," said Mr. Timinson, "then he's no trickster at all."

Kit flexed his paws. He wouldn't let his teacher, his uncle, or his alley down. He would live up to his mother's hopes for him and become the Moonlight Brigadier they wanted him to be.

He tucked the wooden token back inside his hatband. "Let's go."

Chapter Fourteen

THE CARNIVAL OF CROWS

THE Crows' Carnival opened on the first day of the leaf-changing season and went far into the cold days of winter. It was held in a part of the city beneath the Slivered Sky where People rarely gathered, but where they made giant mountains from the things they tossed away.

Declan and the other bats dropped off Kit's class just after sunset that night. All of their bellies were grumbling with hunger, but Mr. Timinson acted like he didn't hear it.

He had to hear it, Kit thought.

"They call this place a dump," Mr. Timinson explained to them as he led the class quickly to a high hedge across the road. "It is a treasure trove for our kind, filled with food and scraps and all manner of useful things, but you will have to resist your natural urges to steal. The crows love a game and a gamble, but they do not take kindly to stealing the way folks in Ankle Snap Alley do. They don't see the fun in it, and they've got long beaks and quick wings. Thieves don't make it out of the carnival with their eyes intact, understood?"

"Understood," said everyone in the class together, as none of them wanted to be pecked to pieces by a carnival of crows.

Mr. Timinson cocked his head at Eeni, whose voice had been strangely absent from the class's response. Kit elbowed her in the side.

"Understood." She shook her head sadly. "What fun is a carnival if you can't pick a pocket or two? We could show back up at home with a few seeds and nuts to spread around."

Kit had to laugh. No matter what bad luck came her way, Eeni was always true to herself: a sneaky little rat with a fearsome streak of loyalty to her neighborhood.

"No stealing. Period," Mr. Timinson said. "The crows can be generous birds, when generosity is shown to them, but with thieves they are cruelest of all the creatures. Not even the Flealess dare steal from crows."

Mr. Timinson sniffed the cold air and watched a single leaf fall, fluttering, from a high branch. Then he peered around a set of trash cans and turned back to the class. "We'll have to cross the street here. We go one at a time. When you see one of those big rolling Rumblers speeding at you, for the good of your guts, do not stop. I can't tell you how many of our animal folk get squashed flat beneath the wheels of Rumblers because they panic in the lights and freeze. Think of this big concrete street like a river. If you stop swimming you'll drown. And of course, by *drown*, I mean 'have your insides flattened against the pavement and your bones pulverized into dust.'"

"Do we really have to cross?" one of the Liney sisters asked nervously.

"I'll help you," Fergus, a frog with a constant bubble of slime on his nose, offered. She scowled at him and whispered with her sisters, giggling.

"You can help me cross," Eeni offered, and the frog smiled.

The Liney sisters rolled their eyes.

"Kit, why don't you go first," Mr. Timinson suggested.

Just then, a roaring Rumbler zoomed by, its terrible tires twirling and kicking up huge clouds of dust and plastic bags behind it. Kit swallowed.

"Don't be scared, Kit," Matteo the church mouse offered. "The night we return to Mother Moon is written already by the Great Scribe's paw. If it's your time to go, then there will be endless feasts of cheese waiting on the other side."

"Uh . . ." Kit didn't take much comfort in the mouse's faith. He'd rather be alive than eat cheese for all eternity.

"I bet the Moonlight Brigade wasn't afraid of crossing a street," Dax the squirrel added, which was a far better argument to get Kit moving.

Mr. Timinson beckoned for Kit to step forward. "When you see there are no Rumblers coming this way or coming that way, you run across, got it? But look both ways first. We aren't deer. We don't just charge across and hope for the best. Always look both ways. If you are careful, you have nothing to fear."

Kit nodded and took a creeping step forward. Then another.

"Go!" Mr. Timinson gave him a shove on the backside, and Kit ran, straight across the wide strip of pavement. Halfway across, he stopped. He'd reached a line that ran down the middle and stretched as far as he could see in either direction. Was it some kind of fence? Some sort of barrier? He sniffed at it.

"Go!" Mr. Timinson shouted. "Go!"

Kit looked back and saw his class staring at him. Dax shifted anxiously from paw to paw, Fergus's neck bulged with every croak, and Eeni waved frantically to urge Kit along. Only Matteo looked relaxed. He winked at Kit.

Kit raised a paw to step across the strange line, hesitated, then saw a Rumbler coming his way. It seemed to be getting bigger and bigger with every instant he looked at it. Its lights blinded him, brighter and brighter.

He realized too late it was a trick of the eyes. The box wasn't growing, it was getting closer very, very quickly. He started to step forward, doubted that he'd make it across in time, then turned to run back the way he'd come, but he froze that way too. Eeni and Mr. Timinson and the rest of his class were shouting at him, but he couldn't hear what they were saying over the deafening roar of the approaching Rumbler. His ears filled with a strange noise, like the honk of a goose, only much louder.

Suddenly, Eeni broke from her hiding spot and charged at him, and Mr. Timinson bolted after her.

"Run!" she yelled.

They ran at Kit. Eeni dove onto Kit's head as Mr. Timinson tackled him from the front. The Rumbler, which it turned out had been making the goose sound, swerved and passed straight over them. Kit looked up to see its underside, all gears and wheels and hot liquids dripping.

The thing was gone almost as soon as it had arrived, zooming along without slowing or coming back to check if it had squashed them.

Mr. Timinson shoved them the rest of the way across the street to the fence around the carnival.

"Well, that was the wrong way to cross a street," he told Kit. "You'll need to get better at that in the future. Wait here while I get the rest of your classmates across."

"Yes, sir," Kit muttered, looking down at his paws, burning with shame.

The embarrassment of needing a rescue in front of everyone might've been worse than getting crushed to death. Heroes didn't need their best friend and their teacher to tackle them. Heroes could cross a street themselves.

Maybe he wasn't the raccoon his mother hoped he'd be. Maybe he wasn't meant to be as great as the Moonlight Brigade, after all. Maybe the time for that kind of hero really was past. Maybe his home and his uncle were doomed because he'd had dreams that were much too grand for such a frightened little raccoon.

Eeni put a paw on Kit's back, but he brushed it off, ashamed.

Once the whole class had made it across, Mr. Timinson led them through a hole under the fence.

They popped up on the other side amid great heaps of the most astounding trash Kit had ever seen. There were piles of metal, heaps of plastic, oozing mountains of food scraps. Empty cans and boxes and crates and bags wafted delicious smells in Kit's direction: sardines and chocolate and pickle juice and cabbage. Scraps of paper fluttered in the breeze, and the moonlight sparkled off shining shards of colored glass more vivid than a rainbow.

Between these great mounds of garbage, a path meandered. This path was the midway of the carnival, where the crows set up their gaming booths and amusement rides. Every sort of creature—light lovers and night dwellers alike—roamed wide-eyed through the midway, awed by the spectacle the crows had created.

Church mice spun on sideways bicycle wheels turned by a tired-looking crow in a dark blue apron. A colony of young weasels whooped and hollered as they ran through a maze of pipes, while a clutch of chickens clutched one another in fright, watching Cecil the Scorpion Tamer. Cecil was a gopher in nothing but a feathered hat who danced around three trained scorpions, using a spork to keep them at bay.

Countless crows watched from above, roosting on their mountains of trash, while more perched inside the booths and others flew this way and that, carrying prizes or sacks of seeds, singing songs, and cheering when a customer won one of their games. They looked friendly enough, but the fox's warning reminded Kit that though the crows had cheerful expressions, their eyes were open for trouble and their beaks were sharp as sunlight.

"Well," said Eeni. "What are we supposed to learn here?"

"First, we eat," Mr. Timinson said, and, with a wave of his paw, summoned over a concession crow. He bought a small bag of Worms 'n' Nuts for every one of his students. Kit noticed his teacher's seed sack wasn't so full either, but maybe he *had* heard all their stomachs grumbling.

While they ate, their teacher gave them their assignment. "Play a game," he said.

"You brought us here to play a game?" Kit complained. "My uncle's been taken hostage! I'm supposed to be saving the alley from coyote! I'm supposed to be robbing the Flealess! Why should I be playing a game?"

Kit sounded angrier than he wanted to, but he couldn't stop himself. His pride still stung. He needed to remind them that he had bigger worries than some school field trip. He was a hero, and he had hero's work to do!

The other students avoided eye contact with him, which made him feel worse.

His teacher folded his paws in front of himself and lowered his head to Kit, speaking low. "Kit, do you know how you will rob the Flealess and save your home?"

"Not yet," Kit mumbled.

"Then this is the perfect time to play," the teacher told

him. "Since the First Animals walked the world, play has been our way to learn. Bear cubs wrestle so that they learn to fight. Foxes stalk butterflies so that they learn to hunt. And raccoons . . ."

"Play games so that they can learn some tricks," Kit said.

"That's right," Mr. Timinson told him. "Play is how we bend the world to our will. Without play, there can be no discovery. And what you need now, young Kit, is a big discovery. The crows scrounge far and wide to have the best prizes in their booths. Perhaps you'll find some inspiration from their collections. The carnival is the classroom of the imagination, you know. But keep your wits about you."

"I always do," said Kit, his confidence returning. Mr. Timinson hadn't given up on him, after all.

"As for the rest of you," Mr. Timinson said. "Play a game you've never played before. Win or lose, it doesn't matter. I want you to play and to tell us all about the game when you're done. Now go!"

He barked once, and the class scurried across the midway looking for serious fun. Kit and Eeni set off together.

"Thanks for saving me from the Rumbler," Kit told her.

"Well, I didn't feel like making a new best friend," she said. "So I figured I'd need to keep you from getting smushed." She smirked at him and flicked her tail from side to side. "So . . . uh . . . any inspiration yet?"

Kit looked all around as they walked among the Crows' Carnival booths. Each booth was made from the discarded junk in the People's dump, but they had transformed it into art. There were colorful canopies crafted from the metal hoods of Rumblers just like the one that had nearly killed Kit. Bright banners hung from these canopies, some decorated with flowers or birds, others with bold patterns, and a few with rough drawings of all sorts of animals, as if the People's artists didn't have enough ideas on their own, they had to steal from the animal folk.

There were booths selling grubs from great buckets, cans full of corn kernels, entire booths filled to bursting with acorn candy and peanut-butter-cricket cakes and more kinds of cheese bits than Kit had ever seen before, even at Possum Ansel's bakery.

"Worms and grubs! Worms and grubs fried fresh today!" a crow called out his ballyhoo, trying to entice a passing company of moles to spend their hard-earned seeds on his treats.

"I got grubs too!" a crazy-eyed crow shouted from his booth directly across the way. "Fried or steamed, sugared or salted! Grubs, grubs, grubs!"

"Oh, stuff your grubs!" the first crow shouted back. "My grubs have twice the flavor at half the price!"

The moles hesitated.

"He lies!" the other crow yelled.

"Only one way to find out for sure," the first crow said. "Try 'em both! If his are better than mine I'll give you a second helping for half the price!"

Kit realized that wasn't a good deal at all, and that the crows were probably working together to get these moles to part with their seeds. It was a quick trick, but it still had all the parts Kit recognized: the Bamboozle, where the crows acted like they were against each other; the Sting, where the moles bought grubs from both of them; and then the Brush-Off, when the moles went away with their bellies full, feeling like they'd gotten a bargain, never knowing they'd been tricked into buying twice as many grubs as they'd wanted in the first place.

Kit admired the crows' trickery.

"Come play the Beetle Bag!" another crow called out to Kit. "Best Beetle Bag in the whole midway! Our prizes are grand, and our prices are low! Bag up some beetles like a crow who's a pro!"

Behind the crow, sitting on shelves at the back of his booth were an assortment of prizes for the winners of the Beetle Bag game. Highest up—and therefore hardest to win—were toys like the ones People gave the Flealess—bones and balls and squeaky shapes; below that there were scraps of glass, bits of ribbon and cloth, shining buttons and keys and all sorts of pretty objects that some folks liked to decorate their nests and burrows with.

Then were combs and bottles and other musical instruments, and below them, easiest to win, were hundreds of cards with different pictures on them. There was one with a church mouse in a thick robe and sandals, a dog posed strongly in a bowler hat, holding a duck in his mouth, a badger with a banner that said the name Constance, and even a drawing of Azban, the First Raccoon, his fingers crossed behind his back as he made a deal with a Person, whose shadow was the only part of him you could see.

"Ancestor cards," Eeni told Kit. "Folks collect 'em for luck or for playing card games with."

Kit nodded. He liked the drawings and might have liked to win the one of Azban, but that wasn't what had caught his eye.

"I've got it!" Kit exclaimed. "I know how I'm going to rob the Flealess!"

"How?" Eeni asked.

Kit pointed to the highest shelf of prizes. "With *that*," he said, and Eeni's little mouth fell open in surprise.

"Oh no," she said. "That's crazy."

"Crazy like a house pet," Kit replied.

Chapter Fifteen

APPRISED OF
A PRIZE

THE game of Beetle Bag was as old as history and twice as crooked.

The rules were simple: The player stands on a bucket and holds a paddle in his paws. The bucket sits opposite a wall with a variety of different-sized bags hanging from it at different heights. The game operator releases the beetles from a cage, and the beetles fly as fast as they can for freedom. The only thing standing in their way is the player with the paddle. It is the player's job to whack the beetles from midair into the bags hanging on the wall. Different bags are worth different points depending on how hard they are to whack a beetle into.

The beetles themselves are wearing tiny pads so the whacks don't hurt them, but they don't like being whacked either and do their best to dodge the player's paddle.

Once in the bag, the beetles are stuck there until the game is done; the crows perfected a kind of paste that keeps the beetles in place. After all the beetles have either flown off or been whacked into a bag, the score is tallied and the prizes distributed.

In professional tournaments, Beetle Baggers played against another player, their paddles dipped in ink, so each beetle was marked by the player who hit it in, but in Carnival Beetle Bag, there was only one player trying to get as many points as possible to win a prize from the shelves. The ancestor cards on the lowest shelf cost twenty points, the musical instruments were higher up and cost fifty, and the best prizes, the Flealess toys and tools, cost over three hundred points.

The prize Kit had his eyes on was on the highest shelf of all. It didn't have a price on it.

Kit spoke to the crow in the carnival booth. "I'll play your game, Mister—?"

"Cawfrey," the crow said. "From a long line of Carnival

Cawfreys. We've run a Beetle Bagging game since the Duke of Dogs barked and Lord Crow flew over the sun. You'd like to play for some of my fabulous prizes?"

"I would," said Kit. "How much to win the one at the top?"

The crow looked to the top shelf, where Kit was pointing. A dog's collar, bright pink with sparkling stones all around it, hung from a nail. The stones caught the moonlight and shot out colorful rays in all directions. A thick leash made of snakeskin was clipped to it.

"Oh, son of Azban," Crawley said. "What do you want with a Flealess thing like *that*?"

"That's my business," said Kit. "Your business is this game." He pulled out his real bag of seeds, all he had left in the world since Coyote's gang had come through the alley. "And I'd like to play it."

"You're the boss." The crow nodded his head once. "A leash and collar, fit for the Flealess. Five hundred points that'll cost you."

"Five hundred!" Eeni objected. "That's almost impossible!"

"Ak-ak!" the crow objected. "Why just last week I saw a church mouse not half your size score twice that high."

"You're talking about Millicent Musculus!" Eeni said. "She's a professional Beetle Bagger!"

The crow fluffed his feathers. "Just saying, almost impossible is still a little bit possible." He turned his head to Kit. "So, you playing or what?"

Kit nodded.

"That's a seed for every beetle," Cawfrey explained. "As many beetles as you think you can bag or seeds you can spend. More seeds mean more beetles means more points. And it'll take some doing to get to five hundred, I'll tell you that for free."

Kit opened his pouch. He had eleven seeds and an acorn, which was worth another ten seeds. He got Eeni's real pouch too, and she had fourteen seeds and two acorns. He saw Mr. Timinson watching him from across the midway and called his teacher over.

"Can I borrow some seeds?" Kit asked. "I need a lot of tries to win what I'm after."

Mr. Timinson looked at the leash and at the collar and then looked back at Kit. "I see you've found some inspiration, after all."

"Yep," said Kit. "That leash and collar are the key to my plan."

"Very clever indeed," his teacher said, and turned over the four seeds he had left after buying them all a snack.

"Four?" Eeni frowned at Mr. Timinson.

"I'm a teacher," the fox said. "It's not quite as profitable as being a pickpocket."

"That's fifty-nine seeds," Kit said, giving every last one to the crow.

"I'll round up and give you sixty beetles to try," Crawley said. "Because I'm a generous fellow."

"I'll believe there's a generous crow when I meet a snake who can tap-dance," Eeni said.

"Snakes don't have feet—" Crawley objected. "Oh. I get it. Ha. Ha."

"Eeni, don't insult the crows," Kit pleaded. "I need this to work."

Eeni frowned. "Do you have any idea how to play Beetle Bag? It's really hard!"

"I know the rules, but I've never played before," said Kit. "But I have to do it. I have to win this! I have to save Uncle Rik!"

"*You* have to?" Eeni said, and wrinkled her nose. She looked like she was mad about something, but Kit couldn't think what. Why should she be mad? He wasn't asking *her* to do anything. She had no reason to be mad. "What if you don't win?" Eeni asked. "These carnival games are rigged. They're almost impossible."

"If I don't win that collar, my plan to save the alley won't work," Kit said. He stretched his legs and shook out his arms. Eeni watched him, her face harder to read than one of Uncle Rik's thick books. "Don't give me that look," Kit told her. "I gotta do this."

"But why does it have to be *you*?" Eeni snapped at him. Was that why she was angry? Did she want to play Beetle Bag?

"It has to be me," Kit explained, "because I volunteered. That's what heroes do. And I know I can do this." He climbed up onto the bucket and looked down at Eeni. "Like the crow said, almost impossible is just a little bit possible."

Chapter Sixteen

BEETLE BAGGING

KIT stood on the bucket and looked over the crowded midway. His classmates had noticed him about to play and gathered to watch. The Liney sisters had already won new bows for their tails at another game, and Fergus the frog stood beside them, trying to make them notice that he'd won himself a matching bow too. Kit felt bad for him. A frog who felt like a rat couldn't have an easy time of it, especially when the rats refused to notice him.

"Bag 'em all, Kit!" Dax the squirrel shouted up at him.

"Quick of Paw, Kit!" Matteo the mouse added.

Kit hadn't really thought about having an audience.

Suddenly, doubt crept in like a burglar, and it opened the door to fear. He was afraid of embarrassing himself again in front of his class, afraid of letting Ankle Snap Alley down, and afraid, most of all, for Uncle Rik, who was in Coyote's clutches because of him.

Fear was like the acorns in a chipmunk's cheeks, Kit thought. Once you started stuffing yourself, you could hold way more than looked possible. You could fill yourself to bursting and still have room for more.

"What happens if I fall off the bucket?" Kit asked the crow.

"Caw! Caw! Caw!" A chorus of crows on the surrounding mountains of garbage laughed.

"If you fall off, you lose," Crawley said. He flew up to Kit with the Beetle Bagging paddle. It was large and metal with a long handle and a flat metal top that smelled like butter and flour.

"It's called a spatula," Mr. Timinson said as Kit took it from the crow.

"Ready?" Crawley asked.

"Not really," said Kit.

The bird ignored him. He fluttered to a lever beside a small box, gripped it in his beak, and pulled.

There was a brief moment of calm, and then the buzzing beetles took flight.

They swarmed at Kit. The first few zoomed right by his nose, so close he could see his own reflection in the shine of their tough-armored bodies. The moment after they whizzed by him, the beetles turned and settled in a neat row along the opposite side of the booth.

They'd been trained! That meant they would do their best not to let him hit them. Kit should've known better. Every game in Ankle Snap Alley was rigged; why should the Crows' Carnival be any different?

"Whack 'em, Kit!" Eeni yelled.

Kit raised the spatula and started swinging. The first beetles he aimed at flew around it easily. The spatula was heavier than it looked, and it was hard to swing. He cranked it back farther and tried to get more speed going, but they dodged that too. His momentum nearly pulled him off the bucket, and he had to do an elaborate twirl to keep from falling.

When he regained his balance, he raised the spatula again. The beetles were still coming, and if he didn't start hitting them into the bags, there wouldn't be enough left. He'd never get to five hundred points.

The beetles could see the flat part of the spatula coming toward them every time, and they just flew around it.

But beetles were dumb! He might not be able to move as fast as them, but he could think much faster. They dodged the spatula when they saw it coming, but what if they didn't see it? He turned it sideways and held it straight up and down. He stood very still. As the beetles flew toward it, all they could see was the thin side. They aimed right past it.

At the last instant, Kit twisted his paws, and the spatula spun. The beetles flew at full speed into the flat part, and they bounced backward into the bags on the wall. Kit realized that by adjusting the angle he twisted the top when they hit it, he could adjust which bag the beetles went into.

With the next beetles, he aimed for the lower bags and the bags on the corners, which were worth the most points.

"Woo-hoo!" Eeni cheered. "You got 'em!"

Kit spun and moved his spatula quickly from side to side, imagining what the beetles saw and where they'd try to fly. He felt, suddenly, as if he and the spatula were one, like it was another tail or an extra claw.

Whack! Whack! Whack!

He smacked beetle after beetle into bag after bag. The stunned beetles buzzed, fought the force of his attack, but it was their own speed that he'd turned against them, bouncing them into the bags.

This must be how a claw-jitsu master felt!

A fifteen-point shot! And a twenty! He missed the fifty-point bag and only got a five, but every point helped.

As he bounced two more beetles off the spatula, he saw

there were only five left flying from the cage. He needed to make them all count, but they split up, three flying high, two flying low.

Okay, Kit, he thought. *It's Quick of Paw time.*

He planted the back of the spatula against the pillar and used it for leverage to vault into the air as high as he could. As he jumped, he spun upside down, just like he'd done with the bats, and he stretched his back legs out, kicking two of the armored beetles straight into bags. He caught the third with a flick of his tail that turned his whole body. In midair, he swung at the two flying below him and whipped them both side by side into the dead-center bag, worth 101 points.

He finished his flip and landed on the bucket on his back paws, using the long spatula for balance.

He wavered.

He wobbled.

He didn't fall.

Instead, he let out a breath and took a dramatic bow.

His classmates burst into applause. This, he thought, was how a hero should feel.

"Well done, kiddo!" a gray-snouted weasel in a baggy suit told him. "You ever want to play in the Pro Beetle Bagging League, you send a finch my way. You've got a future!" He shoved a scrap of bark into Kit's paw:

Garvey Grum
B. B. Scout and Advisor to the Greats

"Uh, thanks," Kit muttered, trying to get through the crowd to the front of the booth again. Crawley had begun to pull the bags off the wall and pluck out the dizzy, dazed beetles inside, counting up the points.

Eeni and Mr. Timinson kept their eyes on him. Crows were known for their clever counting, after all.

"Let's see here," Crawley said. He spoke very fast and moved the beetles around with his beak, keeping the total on his counting board with a piece of chalk in his claw. "Out of sixty beetles, you got twenty-four bagged—not bad at all for a first-timer! That's two in the center one hundred and one for two hundred and two, plus one in the lower center for two, and two below that for twenty together with three on the side at thirteen apiece, and five in the five and one in the twenty-five and four more in the fifteen, plus fifty in the one—CAW! Sorry, I meant one in the fifty, and two more in the twelve and then one and one in the one and one in the none; that's the bag that gives you no points, alas. So let's see. That's a total of . . ." He did some calculating, while Eeni tried to count on her fingers.

Fergus cleared his throat.

"You forgot one," the frog said. "He got twenty-four beetles bagged, but you only tallied the points for twenty-three."

The crow narrowed his eyes at Fergus, and Kit felt the eyes of all the other crows narrowing at the little frog as well. The crow studied his tally, then looked back at the bags.

"I see . . ." The crow's long beak dipped into the bag for fifty points and pulled out the last squirming beetle. "Fifty more. So that's two in the center one hundred and one for two hundred and two, plus one in the lower center for two, and two below that for twenty together with three on the side at thirteen apiece . . ." The crow ran his count again.

Eeni started counting on her fingers once more.

"Four hundred and ninety-eight," Crawley announced and Kit's heart sank. He looked to Fergus, who nodded sadly in agreement, and then to Mr. Timinson, who concurred.

"Two points shy of your prize," Crawley said. "Better luck next time."

"But wait!" Kit pleaded. "It's just two points! Can't we just, like, round the number up again?"

A roar of hoots and whistles burst from the crows on the great mountains of garbage all around the midway.

"Caw! Caw!"

"Ack-a! Ack-a!"

"Young raccoon"—Crawley leaned down so his long beak was practically poking Kit in the nose—"we crows have not been in the carnival business since the sun first shined off a feather by rounding up to *give away* our prizes."

"Well, what about a trade?" Eeni said. "We could bargain for the last two points?"

"Crows do not bargain," Crawley told her, and then turned back to Kit. "You have a very good score, and it is nothing at all to be ashamed of. While you haven't won the collar and leash, you can take your pick from the rest of our finest prizes! How about this bone that squeaks when you bite it? Or this ball that jingles? Cats seem quite fond of this sort of thing."

"I'm not a cat," Kit said. "I'm a raccoon."

"Well, all you furry scurriers look the same to us." Crawley shrugged. "So what'll it be? You could get a comb harp, a whole pack of ancestor cards, *and* this stuffed doll of a raccoon. You could chew on a doll of yourself, eh? That'd cause some talk in your alley! You could be a— what's it?—a *performance artist*."

"I don't want to be a performance artist," said Kit.

"No one ever does." The crow sighed.

"Is there no way I can get the prize I want?" Kit tried

to make his voice sound as pitiful as possible, but Crawley was unmoved.

He saw that the crow had an interesting little collection of items on the back of his booth, thimbles and buttons and shiny objects that weren't on display with the prizes. It gave Kit an idea. "Can I have one of those?" he pointed.

"Oh no!" Crawley cawed. "That's my private collection. Gifts that have been given to me over the seasons. Some folks are generous with old Crawley."

Kit got an idea, like a firefly lighting up in his brain. He knew what to do, but that didn't mean he wanted to do it.

"Well, I suppose I could add to your collection too, seeing the fun we've had," he said. He reached up into the inside band of his hat and pulled out the wooden token Uncle Rik had given him, the one that had belonged to his mother. He looked at it once more against his paw, the pale brown and light pink. The paws within the paws. He squeezed it once and imagined it passing from his mother's paw to his uncle's, from his uncle's to his and then . . . and then he tossed it to the crow. "That's an antique," he said. His voice cracked as it came out, and he sniffed back the tears he was feeling. "Enjoy it."

The crow caught the token in his beak, set it on the counter, and studied it. Other crows gathered around to look, as crows like nothing more than a gift, especially an antique.

"Bye, Brother Crawley!" Kit called, and turned to leave the booth. He didn't want the crow to see him cry.

"What are you doing?" Eeni asked Kit. "That was your mom's! Why'd you give it away? And you didn't even take a prize!"

"Like Mr. Timinson said," Kit told her. "*The crows can be generous birds, when generosity is shown to them.*"

Mr. Timinson chuckled. "You're gambling on your teacher's wisdom, Kit," he said.

"Seems a safe bet," Kit replied. "Anyway, sometimes you have to lose something you want to make room for something you need."

"A philosopher raccoon." Mr. Timinson smiled.

Kit shrugged. "Just a guy who's lost a lot and lived to learn from it."

"Wait!" Crawley called out as he fluttered down in front of Kit.

"You gave this beautiful token without demanding anything in return," Crawley said, bowing. "Even after your favor was denied to you."

Kit shrugged. "My mom always told me generosity isn't about who deserves it, but about who's able to give it."

Crawley nodded, let out a high screech, and suddenly another crow in a blue apron fluttered down beside him, the leash and collar in his beak.

"I will treasure the gift you have given me," the crow

said. "And I would like to give you this gift. Not in return, but in appreciation."

The other crow set the leash and collar down on the ground.

Kit picked it up and bowed his head to the crow.

"Thank you, gentle crow," he said.

"The blessings of the high winds and clear skies upon you, son of Azban," said Crawley, then bowed to Eeni. "And to you, daughter of the Great Mother Rat." He gave a sly look to Mr. Timinson, but didn't bow. He and the other crow simply flew back to their gaming booth and began their ballyhoo again, trying to rope in more customers to their game.

Thanks, Ma, Kit thought to himself. *Thanks for being there, even when you're not.*

"I can't believe that worked," said Eeni.

The class gathered around their teacher. "All of One Paw," said Mr. Timinson. "You see now, how knowing something about all sorts of creatures can give you an advantage? Kit has demonstrated this well tonight. Your next assignment is simple. Find your own way home." He gave Kit a raised-eyebrow look. "Without getting crushed beneath a Rumbler."

Eeni took Kit's paw. "I'll get him across the street alive."

"Very good," said Mr. Timinson. "Until tomorrow night, then."

"Tomorrow night's the coyote's deadline," said Kit.

"I am aware," said Mr. Timinson. His whiskers twitched, and his yellow eyes watched Kit closely.

"So . . . uh . . . ," Kit thought aloud. "I'm not sure I can come to school."

"Because you have to save the alley?" the fox asked.

"That's right," Kit said.

"All by yourself?"

"I made the deal," Kit told him.

The fox shook his head. "All of One Paw," he said mysteriously, and trotted off without another word to the class.

Kit set the leash and collar down and dipped his paws in a puddle to wash them in the cold water. He stared down at his reflection. The raccoon looking back up at him looked heroic enough. He took off his hat and smoothed the fur between his ears.

He had a plan now, but it was dangerous and it could go wrong in more ways than a tree had leaves. But it was his plan, and it was clever and brave as any the First Raccoon ever came up with in the stories of the Moonlight Brigade.

"What do you need that leash and collar for?" Fergus asked him. The snot bubble on his nose popped. The others gathered around behind him.

"What's the difference between us and the Flealess?" Kit asked them in return.

"We're free," Matteo said. "And those spoiled pets live in luxury as prisoners of their People."

"Just a bunch of leash lovers, they are," Dax added.

"Exactly," said Kit. "They've got leashes and we don't. Except—"

"Now we do!" Matteo finished his thought. "So you're gonna pretend to be some Person's pet?"

Kit nodded.

"That *is* a crazy plan."

"I really hope you know what you're doing," Eeni said, picking up the prize to study it.

He carefully took it from her paws.

He really hoped he did too. Everything depended on him and him alone.

Chapter Seventeen

WHAT DOES THE FOX SAY?

HE'S doing well," Mr. Timinson whispered into the shadow of the water tower on the school rooftop, watching the sky turn red with the sunrise. "But he has not realized the truth of the Moonlight Brigade yet."

"You did well guiding him," a voice in the shadows responded, a voice that seemed to be young and old, high and deep, male and female, a hundred voices in one voice. Beneath the sound of its words, there was a gnawing sound, like a thousand teeth chewing at once. The rising light caused two hundred eyes to shine like stars, before the creature recoiled deeper into darkness. "But you mustn't let him think you will be there to help him again."

"But what if he needs help?" said one rat voice in the tangle of rats that made the Rat King.

"He will have to learn to ask for it," said another.

"We've given him all the help he needs already," said a third. *"He simply has to notice it."*

"If the plural of foot *is* feet, *why isn't the plural of* root, *reet?"* wondered a fourth.

The fox waited patiently for the Rat King to finish arguing with itself.

One of the difficulties of being the Rat King was that its thoughts were the conversation among the individual rats who comprised it, so anyone standing near the Rat King could hear what they were thinking all the time. That was one of the reasons that Rat King liked to be alone. Anyone would sound crazy if they had to say every passing thought they had out loud.

"But time is short and we need to be ready," the Rat King said at last.

"Are we perhaps expecting too much from a raccoon his age?" the fox asked. "Perhaps your vision is clouded by . . ." The fox stopped himself.

"By *what* do you think our vision is *clouded*?" the Rat King hissed.

"By sentimentality," the fox said. "We know your relationship to Eeni."

"We have no relationship to Eeni," the Rat King answered, though the fox could detect a certain hesitation in the tone of voice. "When a rat joins us, she forswears all previous ties to friends and family, vows to serve only the wild. And so our love for Eeni is no different from our love for any other free creature."

The fox would not argue with the Rat King, but his eyes searched the shadowy mass of entangled rats for the one who had been Eeni's mother.

Clever as he was, he still couldn't tell which she was.

"Will you stay in hiding until this is over?" he asked the Rat King.

"We must," the Rat King answered. "The owls are hunting us. Coyote was clever to bring them."

"It is a dangerous game we're making Kit play," Mr. Timinson said. "We told Coyote about the First Frost Festival. We knew he would come. Perhaps we shouldn't have brought someone so dangerous?"

"It was the only way to know if this was the time for the Moonlight Brigade to return," the Rat King said. "Greatness does not reveal itself without great challenge."

"But what if he does not succeed? What if we are wrong?"

"Then he will be beyond worry," said the Rat King.

"Because he will have surely been eaten. But we have faith."

"And you can live with that?" Mr. Timinson asked. "You can gamble the destruction of an innocent raccoon and of all the creatures of Ankle Snap Alley on a little faith?"

"Did you hear that?" one rat said.

"He called Kit innocent?" another said.

"Not that," said a third. *"He called it a little faith?"*

The Rat King's voice spoke once more as one. "There is nothing little about faith," it declared, and then fell silent.

The fox crept forward and climbed into the water tower. It was empty. The Rat King had gone. The air still hung heavy with their scent of the city and the sewers and the hungry breath of a hundred rats.

Alone in the rooftop water tower, he found himself speaking aloud the very words that were, at that moment, echoing through Kit's thoughts in his uncle's empty apartment back in Ankle Snap Alley: "I really hope you know what you're doing."

Chapter Eighteen

DANGER TOES

WHAT am I doing? Kit asked himself.

He had stayed up all day with Uncle Rik's thick books, reading from the moment the sun came up until it began to sink again, putting together all the details of the trick he was going to pull. Eeni'd fallen asleep curled in his tail and she was snoring quietly in the dim light of dusk.

Uncle Rik was a historian, and he had volumes and volumes of books in his house, books Kit had never bothered to read before. They were written in the tiny writing of the mice and had titles like

Tales of Azban in the Age of the New(ish) Moon, as told to the Mice of Hedgerow Parish.

Mousekind Saves the City: True Tales of Heroic Rodents by Rev. H. H. Musculus Jr.

A History of Dogs: Why They Sniff, Snore, and Snarl by Brother Mesrick M. Mawmouth, the Fourth.

Kit spent the final moments of the day studying the dog book, memorizing every scrap of information he could. He couldn't solve his problems with brute strength, not against Coyote and not against the Flealess. He had to use his smarts, which meant he had to get more smarts quickly, and like his uncle said, "Reading a book is like stealing the smarts of the author. It's the fastest way to lift a lifetime of learning without leaving your seat."

Except Kit had to leave his seat now. He slipped quietly from his bed of moss and feather and soft scraps of paper, easing his tail out from under Eeni and yawning so wide he could have swallowed her whole. But sleep would have to wait. He crept to the window, pulling aside the tattered sash and peering into Ankle Snap Alley, where the creatures had begun to stir for the night.

There was, as ever, a line in front of Possum Ansel's, but the possum himself, with Otis at his side, was in the midst of shooing the creatures away, explaining he had nothing to sell them, that the otters had ransacked his business and taken everything.

The story was the same all over. The coyote's gang had stolen every scrap they could carry. They'd tossed furniture into the thoroughfare, tossed the church mice's printing press into the Dumpster, and even tossed the seats from the van where the Rabid Rascals lived.

The Blacktail brothers had gone with the otters, and no one else had the heart to take their place running a scam on the corner. It was a sad day in Ankle Snap Alley when even the gambling and cheating came to a stop. The coyote hadn't just stolen their seeds and nuts; he'd stolen the mischievous spark that made the place special. He'd stolen its pride.

"The neighborhood's a mess," Eeni said, surprising Kit at his side. At its best Ankle Snap Alley had been a ragged place, but now it was barely fit for living things. When the real cold of winter came, there'd be no way to live in it. The thought gave Kit a chill.

"They're all counting on me," he said.

Eeni grunted.

"What?" Kit whirled on her. "Why are you so mad at me?"

"You keep talking about yourself!" she said. "You keep talking about what *you* have to do, and what plans *you* have to save everyone."

"Yeah," snapped Kit. "*I* made the deal with Coyote. It's *my* responsibility."

"You keep saying that," Eeni told him. "But for a

fella who wants to do well in school, you sure don't pay attention."

"What do you mean?"

"You still haven't figured it out? What All of One Paw means? Why it was the motto of the Moonlight Brigade?"

Kit shrugged. He hadn't really thought about it since the first night of school.

"It means as long as you walk this earth with your paws underneath you, you ain't alone," Eeni snapped.

"I am, though!" Kit snapped back at her. "I got my uncle into this trouble. Coyote came to the alley because of me! He said so himself. I can't ask anyone else to risk their hides for me anymore."

"Wouldn't be the first time," said Eeni. "Anyway, if I stuck my head under a rock every time you roped me into trouble, I'd have a snout full stones by now."

"I won't let anyone else get hurt," said Kit. "It's bad enough what I put Uncle Rik through. It's too dangerous."

"I'm not afraid of danger. I chew the toes off danger."

"Danger has toes?"

"It's just a saying," said Eeni.

"I've never heard that saying before," said Kit.

"I just said it!"

Kit set his jaw and told her, "I have to do this myself. I have to be the hero. I owe it to—"

"You don't owe it to anyone," Eeni cut him off. "Not to Mr. Timinson or to Uncle Rik, not even to your mother!"

"Yes, I do!" Kit yelled back.

"She's gone!" Eeni yelled at him.

"At least she didn't abandon me!"

Kit knew he'd gone too far. So did Eeni. Their words had hit each other harder than a punch in the snout. No one could hurt you the way your friends could, and Kit really wished he could unsay what he'd said. But that wasn't how words worked. You can't ungrowl a growl. What gets barked, stays barked.

"I'm sorry, Eeni," Kit whispered. "But I do owe it to my mother. She died saving me so that I could do something great with my life. Being a hero like the Moonlight Brigade is exactly what I need to do."

Eeni bit her lip. She ground her teeth. She looked like she was about to say something, then stopped herself. Outside, the cloud of bats started to swirl above the darkening sky, swooping in to pick the kids up for school.

"You should go to school," Kit said. "No reason for both of us to miss."

Eeni let out a sigh. "And what'll you be doing?" She was still whispering, like the air around them was fragile as the frost on a leaf and too loud a noise might crack it. But they both knew it wasn't the air that was fragile right then. It was their feelings. It was their friendship.

"I'll be sneaking into a Flealess house," Kit told her. "And pulling off a trick that'll save our alley."

"All alone?"

"All alone," said Kit.

Eeni shook her head. "You may be a great trickster," she said, "but you're still a rube." She grabbed her vest and put it on, stomping out the door.

"Eeni, wait!" Kit called after her.

She raised her paws, and the bats hoisted her into the sky.

"Eeni!" Kit shouted. "Don't be mad at me! I'm trying to protect you!"

She didn't answer him, and he was all alone.

Friends were so confusing. She was mad at him because he didn't want her to get hurt? What kind of sense did that make?

Kit shook his head as he closed the door and took off his jacket. He couldn't worry about Eeni right now. He had work to do.

He had a heist to pull.

Chapter Nineteen

AN INSIDE JOB

THE sun had set and the disk of the moon cast its milky light over the city. Kit scurried across the streets outside of Ankle Snap Alley, running to the doorway of the last house where a raccoon like himself would be welcome.

The leash trailed behind him like a deflated snake nipping at his neck. The collar made him itch, and he fought the urge to tear it off. The Flealess were comfortable in their collars, and he needed to look like one of them. He arrived at the front steps that led from the sidewalk to a tall blue door. There was a shining metal knocker and little hole above it for People to peep out from.

As he climbed the steps, he thought how little he really knew about People and their house pets but how much of his trick depended on them doing what he thought they would do. He found himself wishing he could ask his uncle for advice. Danger felt so much less scary when there was someone waiting for you to come home at the end of it.

But his home was empty, and if he was going to have a home to come back to, he had stay brave.

"Quick of Paw and Slick of Tongue, Brave of Heart, Afraid of None," he whispered to himself. "A Friend to All in Need of One."

He stood up on his back paws and stretched as high as he could. With his front claws, he scratched on the door, making as much noise as possible. There was a quiet moment. He scratched again to make sure whoever was inside heard him.

And then the barking erupted.

"WHO'S THERE? SOMEONE'S THERE! GET THE DOOR, GET THE DOOR, GET THE DOOR!" the dog inside yelled. Kit heard the People say something and the barking stopped. The door swung open, and one of the giant People stood in front of him, looking around over his head. The Person said something and then looked down and saw Kit. The Person nearly jumped out of its hairless skin at the sight. Kit immediately made the most pitiful face he could make and held his leash up in in his paws. "I'm lost," he said. "I lost my People."

Of course, the Person didn't speak his language, just like he didn't speak the Person's. He decided to make whatever sad noises he could think of, all while shoving the leash up at the Person. The leash was his message. The leash was his plea. The Person had to believe the leash or else Kit would never get inside the house. As much as he wanted to tear off the collar and throw the leash into the dirt, screaming his freedom with a mighty growl, he couldn't.

He kept showing the Person that leash. This was their Bamboozle. They had believe it. Another Person came to the door, speaking, but they dropped into heavy silence the moment they saw Kit.

"Please," Kit said again, his tone so sad and desperate he almost believed his own lie. He brought tears to his eyes. They were "crocodile tears."

Crocodiles were lovers of fine food, and they only cried when they ate an especially delicious victim, so the saying had been born that fake tears were crocodile tears.

Kit knew, if his victims were to take him inside, he had to cry twice as convincingly as any crocodile ever had.

"I lost my People!" he wailed. "Look! They dropped my leash. This is my leash that my People put on me. Please help. Oh, woe is me! I am a lost Flealess house pet who needs your help! Pretty please let me in to safety! There are wild animals outside who will eat me up! Please, oh, pretty please!"

Behind the People, the dog peered around, and when he saw Kit, he growled a deadly, gut-rumbling growl.

"You!" said the dog in a gruff, booming voice. "What are *you* doing here?"

"Hey, Titus. Been a long time," said Kit to the dainty silver dog, a miniature greyhound who had been the leader of the Flealess when they'd tried to destroy Ankle Snap Alley. This was the dog who'd ordered Kit's parents eliminated. This was the dog who'd sent an assassin after Eeni. This was the dog who'd happily see every last rat and raccoon in the wide world wiped away.

This was the dog on whom Kit's entire plan depended.

Titus, enraged, charged at Kit, barking wildly. "I'll rip you to shreds, you filthy gutter-guzzling grub grabber!"

Kit flinched and dove sideways, nearly falling down the stairs back onto the street. He curled into a ball, covering his head with his paws and shaking with fright. He shook enough so the People saw him shake, and he braced himself for the feel of Titus's teeth tearing his skin.

But the bite never came. He glanced out from under his black paws and saw one of the People holding the dog back by the collar, scolding him.

Kit hid his smile and then went back to pleading. "Oh,

please protect me from your dog," he cried. "I'm just a lost Flealess myself."

"Oh, quiet, Kit!" Titus barked. "Feeders don't understand a word we animal folk say. What game are you playing here?"

"Make them take me in," Kit said. "And I'll explain."

"I can't make my Feeders do anything," Titus said. "Except feed me . . . and groom me. And walk me and play with me and pick up my poo . . . and . . . well, I can't make them take you inside! I won't!"

"I see." Kit sighed. "I guess you Flealess really are as helpless as you look. No wonder we defeated you so easily the last time we met."

Titus snarled. "We were *not* defeated. The Flealess will never be defeated! We agreed to a truce. The Feeders—or People, like you call them—and their houses are ours and that filthy alleyway belongs to you. But now, you have come here! You are breaking our truce, and I *will* call the council together. We *will* declare war on every last one of you again. There *won't* be a pigeon left to chew on your bones when we're through!"

"Those are big words for a puppy whose front paws can't even touch the ground," Kit replied. Titus noticed for the first time that his People were holding him back so hard that the front half of his body was off the ground and his paws were clawing at the air.

He stopped struggling and allowed himself to be set back down. His People still held him by the collar, though. They were talking to each other, pointing down at Kit, and talking more. He still wasn't sure they'd let him inside.

"They think you have Foaming Mouth Fever," said Titus.

"You understand them?"

"I know a few words of their language," said Titus.

"Can they understand you?"

"Ha!" Titus laughed. "No animal folk can talk to them. They've *learned* not to understand us. But one thing they all know is the difference between a pet and a *pest*. And you, Kit, are a pest. Feeders don't take in raccoons. I can't wait to see them kick you to the—HEY! WHAT ARE YOU DOING?" He barked furiously at his People as one of them dragged him from the door and hauled him up the stairs, slamming the door to some upper room.

The other Person grabbed Kit's leash and tugged him into the house.

At first, he resisted. A raccoon does not like to be pulled, but then he remembered he was supposed to be a Flealess raccoon, so he let himself be dragged. Before he knew what was happening, the People had taken him into a room that smelled like more foods than Kit had ever smelled in his life. They had fruits and vegetables in a bowl on a table, sitting out, a leap and swipe of the paw away.

But Kit didn't have the chance to swipe any of it. They

had a cage on the floor of this room, and they shoved him into it, unclipping the leash and closing the latch. Inside, he had a cushion and some toys that smelled like Titus, along with a bowl of water. He looked up at the People and one of them shoved a bone-shaped snack into the cage. It had a peanut butter scent. Kit took it from the Person with his paws, and the Person laughed.

They watched him wash his treat in the water bowl. The other one came back, and they talked in their weird words. What would they do to him? They could let him stay or toss him out. Or they could bring over the Bagman, the one who collected animal folk from the traps and vanished them into his sack, never to be seen again.

The People had lots of choices on how to handle Kit if they didn't believe he was a lost Flealess house pet.

Kit realized, perhaps too late, that there were far too many ways for his plan to go wrong. It was like walking across a thin branch over a deep ravine: a thousand ways to fall but only one narrow way to climb.

He needed a miracle, and he spoke an old raccoon plea to his ancestor:

"First Raccoon, oh First Raccoon,
please aid your friend beneath the moon.
Although my claws are small and grasping,
grant this hope that I am asking:

If I should meet with any foes,
confound their sight and trip their toes,
and if I should need to speak a lie,
please give it wings that it may fly.
As mischief is your sacred game,
I do my mischief in your name."

The People stared at him. Although they could not have known his words, there are three things all creatures understand in whatever language they are spoken: the sound of a broken heart, a joyful laugh, and a desperate prayer.

Kit had stirred their sympathy. The People murmured quietly to each other and left the room, bathing it in lovely darkness by touching a switch on the wall. He didn't know what would come next, but it appeared he'd won the People's trust and would get to stay in the house for the night.

Or at least until he escaped.

He peered up from the cage and through the rear window, which looked out on Ankle Snap Alley. He knew the cold night was coming on, but he was warm inside. In the dark of the alley outside, he could make out three shapes, three shadows perched atop the fence that blocked the People's yard from Ankle Snap Alley. Six yellow eyes blinked down upon him.

He did his best to look comfortable in the cage. He knew the owls could see him inside the Flealess house. He *needed* them to see him inside the Flealess house, so he did what he imagined Eeni would do in his place. Probably something insouciant.

He winked at them.

The owls swiveled their heads to look at one another. Then one of them flapped her wings, launched from her perch, and flew away, no doubt to tell the coyote that Kit was inside a Flealess house.

So far, everything was going as Kit had planned. He said his silent thanks to the First Raccoon, and he settled in to wait for the People to go to sleep. Once they slept, the house would belong to him, and he had some unfinished business with the dog upstairs.

Chapter Twenty

PAW-TO-PAW COMBAT

TIME passed slowly while Kit waited to make his move. Something hanging on the wall clicked over and over again, the same beat endlessly.

Ticktock ticktock ticktock ticktock.

How very dull People music was, thought Kit. And strange they let it play while they slept.

A tall metal box beside the cage hummed, and cool air seeped from its door. There was a hiss of hot air from a vent in the floor. The People's house was filled with all sorts of devices that made all sorts of strange noises.

Kit could imagine how much his uncle Rik would enjoy being in here, investigating the objects and encouraging Kit to dismantle them. Kit was good at taking things apart, springing open traps, using his quick mind and nimble fingers to solve tricky problems. But what if he'd talked his way into a problem he couldn't solve? What if this wasn't a story about him being a hero, but about him getting his uncle hurt, making his best friend mad, and failing, in the end, to save anyone?

He sat back on his tail and wanted to cry. He wanted to howl. He wanted to shake his cage and scream at the moon that it was all so unfair!

But screaming wouldn't help him. Only he could help himself now.

His fingers went to work, stretching through the wire of the cage, grabbing the latch, and slipping the lock. The People must not have known much about raccoons to put him in such a flimsy cage.

He pushed the door open and stepped into the big room, taking a deep breath of freedom. He smiled. He was a raccoon at large in a Flealess house, and he hadn't even needed to break in. He'd been invited.

"You were safer in the cage," Titus's voice rumbled from behind an island of cabinets. He stepped around into a streak of moonlight. "But I knew you'd be out as soon as my Feeders went to bed. And once you *were* out, I knew I could rip you to shreds."

"Now, Titus." Kit held up his paws. "If you attack me, won't your People be angry at you? I'm under their protection now."

"Ha!" said Titus. "My *Feeders* couldn't care less about you. They've already called for the Bagman to come get you in the morning."

Kit gulped, and Titus laughed.

"Oh yes, you know what the Bagman is. Do you know what happens when he gets you? He sends you down for the long nap, the last snore, and it's good-bye, Kit. None of my kind will shed a single tear and none of yours will ever know what became of you."

"But . . . but your People took me in?" Kit sounded frightened now. "They can't just turn me over to the Bagman."

Titus shrugged. "They won't get a chance. I'm going to finish you off first!"

The dog leaped at Kit, and nothing held him back this time. His tough teeth snapped on empty air as Kit jumped from the floor to the top of the cabinets, sliding across the smooth stone surface. He nearly sent the bowl of delicious-smelling fruit clattering to the floor, but he caught it before it fell. He didn't want to wake the People. They might come to his rescue, but they'd ruin his plans.

Titus tried to jump onto the countertop after Kit, but couldn't reach. Kit noticed that he wasn't barking. He didn't want his People to come to Kit's rescue either.

"Get down here," Titus whispered. "Get down here and fight me properly!"

"Fight you?" Kit whispered. "I'm just a kid, and you're a trained dog. I could never dream of fighting you. I need your help. Aren't we all animals of the city? Friend or foe, don't we want to protect our home from invasion by fearsome predators from the Big Sky country?"

"Ha!" said Titus. "You came from the Big Sky country!"

"But I'm hardly fearsome," Kit said.

"You've got that right," Titus said, laughing. "You were brave coming to me to try to save your alley, but there is a whisker-thin line between bravery and foolishness. I fear that you, Kit, are more foolish than brave coming here alone. You've put yourself in terrible danger."

Kit smirked and thought of Eeni. "I chew the toes off danger," he said.

Titus cocked his head. "Danger has toes?"

"It's a famous saying," Kit told him. "Listen, Titus, I know I risked my life coming here. I don't want to fight."

"What *do* you want, then?" the dog asked, still circling him with fangs bared.

"Simple," said Kit. "I want your food."

"My food?" Titus stopped circling. "I don't understand."

"I want the cans of food your People feed you," Kit said.

"You've been hanging out with bats, haven't you?" Titus asked. "It seems you're becoming a comedian."

"This is no joke," said Kit. "Give me your food, and I'll owe you a big favor."

"I don't want your favors," Titus told him.

Time for another Bamboozle, Kit thought. He'd never expected Titus to help him, but he knew a thing or two about dogs now, thanks to Uncle Rik's books, and he knew exactly what he could get this dog to do. "I demand you apologize for the insults you have hurled against the Wild Ones," he told Titus. "I demand you face justice for the murder of my parents!"

"I didn't murder your parents," said Titus.

"But you are responsible for it," said Kit. "If you won't apologize, then I demand you face me in a Dog's Duel."

"You're not a dog," Titus objected.

"There's no rule that I have to be," said Kit. "I read every rule there is. I've challenged you by the rules set forth in the days of Brutus, Duke of Dogs, and I demand you answer my challenge!"

Titus panted in thought. "Very well, Kit. I accept. It's a duel."

Suddenly, a large gray parrot seized Kit from behind. Two hamsters burst from hiding places beneath the sink and bound his paws with the laces from People's shoes, and two Siamese cats slid like twin ghosts from the shadows, two sets of razor-sharp teeth shining side by side.

"Oh, I forgot to mention I'd invited some friends over," said Titus.

Kit struggled against the parrot's grip, but its talons dug deeper into his shoulders. "Let me go, you big dumb bird!"

"You shouldn't insult Byron," Titus said. "He doesn't say much when his Feeders aren't around. He lets his talons do the talking, if you know what I mean."

Kit stopped struggling. He glanced at the window and saw the outline of the remaining two owls watching his struggles through the window.

As he was hauled down to his belly in front of Titus, one of the owls flew from her perch to carry the message to the coyote that Kit was now a prisoner.

Good, thought Kit. *Everything's going just like I thought it would.*

All he had to do now was defeat a dog in a Dog's Duel.

As far as Kit's book said, no raccoon since Azban ever had.

Chapter Twenty-One

DOG'S DUEL

A Dog's Duel, like a Raccoon's Trick, has three parts. The first is the Growl of Challenge, where one dog (or raccoon), feeling himself wronged in some way, demands justice. When justice is denied, the duel is declared.

This begins the second part, the Barking of Oaths. Each dog, having accepted the duel, vows an oath to honor the results of the duel, burying their quarrel when the duel is done, whatever the results.

And the third part, the final part, is the Pull.

The dogs face each other at ten strides, gripping opposite ends of a tough rope in their jaws. In the center between them sits the Skunk Puddle, a puddle filled with sticky tar, skunk spray, and chili powders. The Fleahess trade with all kinds of creatures to assemble their supplies, which is how the crows came to have so many Fleahess prizes in their booths.

Any unfortunate creature who set even a single paw in the Skunk Puddle becomes so terribly trapped and so impossibly stinky, not even the foulest garbage-dwelling worm would want to get close him. The only way to get free from the sticky trap is to beg the winner to shave off all the loser's fur and let him go. The chili powder makes the whole process hurt worse than a wasp's sting.

If a duelist lets go of the rope to avoid falling into the puddle, however, he forfeits instantly, and the audience rolls him in the puddle themselves. The winner doesn't even have to set him free, no matter how much he begs. He's left to lie there until the ants pick his bones dry.

To put it plainly, Kit did not want to lose this duel.

"I, Titus, vow before this audience of Fleahess that I will respect the results of this duel," Titus said.

They had slipped out of the People's house single file through the doggy door and gathered in the yard. The other house pets stood in a circle around the dueling field to block any chance of Kit's escape.

"When our duel is done"—Titus couldn't hide a smile from his face—"I will shave this garbage-grubbing raccoon and set him free *only* if he leaves his beloved Ankle

Snap Alley forever. I am tired of seeing him every evening through my window."

Kit bit his lip. If he lost, he'd not just lose his fur. He'd lose his home.

Then again, if he lost, he'd lose his home to Coyote before he could ever go into the exile Titus was demanding.

"Very well," said Mr. Peebles, a hamster and the master of the duel. He bowed to Titus. He turned to Kit at the other end of the rope, which lay in front of him in the grass like a snake braced to bite. "What say you?"

"I, Kit, uh, vow . . ." He didn't really know what he was supposed to say. Everything he knew about the Dog's Duel, he'd learned from his uncle's book that very day, and the author hadn't been very specific on this point. Why couldn't authors put in everything their readers might need to know? Didn't they realize some folks might come to rely on their books for survival?

Kit did his best to repeat what Titus had said. "I vow before this audience of Flealess that I will respect the results of this duel. When I win—" At this, his oath was interrupted by a roar of laughter from the crowd. "*When I win*," Kit repeated more loudly, "I will shave Titus's fur and set him free only if he promises me every can of Flealess food that I can carry."

"The oaths are made!" Mr. Peebles declared. "Duelists, take the rope!"

Titus bent his head and took his end of the rope in his jaws. Kit picked it up with his paws. He braced his back claws in the dirt and prepared himself to pull with every ounce of strength he had.

He'd studied the rules for hours and hours but studying a thing and doing a thing were quite different, and he sure hoped all his dreaming and scheming wouldn't end in a stinking puddle of painful sludge.

The Skunk Puddle shined in the moonlight.

From the other side of the fence, the last owl sister watched the scene. If Kit lost, she'd fly to Coyote to tell him right away that Kit had failed to rob the Flealess, and Uncle Rik's life wouldn't be worth the dirt in a mole's nose. Kit would never see his uncle again, and he would never see Ankle Snap Alley again either.

Also, he'd have all his fur shaved off just as the winter winds blew in.

He shivered.

If he lost, he'd have lost everything and everyone and he was pretty sure that was a loss he'd never bounce back from. There was only so much losing a fella could do before he lost himself too. Maybe he'd end up like Coyote and start robbing from those who were weaker than he or maybe he'd end up like Titus and try to destroy any folk who were different from him.

He didn't like any of those visions of his future, so he figured he better not lose.

"Duelists!" the hamster shouted, snapping Kit's attention back to the present moment. "Duel!"

Titus tugged, and Kit felt like his arms were being ripped out of his shoulders. He lurched forward, stumbling and nearly falling on his face. The rope slipped. He almost dropped it.

Another dog in the crowd cheered. "Go, Titus! Make that raccoon regret he ever tangled with the Flealess!"

Kit tried to pull, but his claws were slipping. The rope dragged him forward, closer and closer to the puddle. He could smell the bitter skunk stench and the hot chili burn looming ahead.

He heaved backward, slowing his slide, but not stopping it. The dog was stronger than he was. There was no way he could out-dog Titus. Dogs trained their whole lives at tugging.

Kit's paws scrambled helplessly. He pulled harder, but the rope kept moving the other way. His muscles burned, his bones ached. The unfriendly faces of the animals around him cheered his slow slide toward doom.

He slipped another step, stumbled on a stone, his grip loosed, and it took all his strength to hold the rope. Titus snarled. His lips quivered. He jerked his head this way and that, shaking Kit from side to side.

He would not lose by forfeit. He would *not* drop the rope, no matter the agony.

"Quick of Paw and Slick of Tongue, Brave of Heart, Afraid of None, a Friend to All in Need of One." He said the words of Azban, the First Raccoon, through gritted teeth. He looked around the crowd, and saw not a friendly face among them.

He was the one who needed a friend right now, but he was all alone.

Why hadn't he let Eeni come with him? Why had he insisted on being a lone hero? He'd told her it was to keep her safe, but she never wanted safety. She wanted respect. She wanted to be treated like a friend. She wanted to help.

And *that* was what All of One Paw meant. Eeni hadn't gotten it right when she said it was about every creature being the best version of themselves. That was only part of it. All of One Paw really meant that every creature was stronger with others than he was on his own. A little paw couldn't do much by itself, but a hundred paws together, all with different shapes and sizes . . . they could do *anything*. The Moonlight Brigade wasn't just one hero. It was a community, all different folk, all together.

Kit was so close to the puddle that its fumes burned his nostrils.

He slid another stride. He could see his reflection in the rippling surface of the gruesome goo. Two more tugs from Titus, and he'd fall in. Kit's own face stared up at him, tears on his cheeks. And behind him, high above, the glimmer of the moon. *His* moon. The raccoon moon.

This was a Dog's Duel, but a raccoon's night. He couldn't win against a dog's strength. He could only win with a raccoon's wits.

And he knew what to do.

He had a new plan.

"You're going in," Titus growled through his teeth around the rope, and braced his paws for another pull. Kit cocked his head to the side and gave Titus one little insouciant wink.

As he winked, he also relaxed, let himself be pulled forward. The sudden slack in the rope made Titus stumble backward as he tugged. The dog fell, and as he fell, he lost his grip on the rope.

"Forfeit!" Mr. Peebles cried. "Titus has released the rope!"

Kit exhaled with relief, panting in place over the puddle, stilling holding the rope with raw and burning paws.

"No!" Titus yelled. "I . . . I didn't . . . He . . . he cheated!" Titus turned, facing the audience. "He stopped tugging."

"There's no rule he has to tug," Mr. Peebles explained. "Only that he hold the rope . . . and as you see, he still is."

Titus shook. His whole body quivered. The other Flealess closed in on him. The parrot, Byron, seized Titus's collar. The Siamese cats flanked him. The other dogs bared their teeth at their former friend.

"It is our way," said Mr. Peebles. "You accepted the duel and lost it. You go in the puddle at Kit's command. He is the winner."

At the announcement, the last of the keen-eared owls flew off to tell the good news to Coyote. Kit had won all the Flealess food he could carry.

Kit stepped back from the disgusting puddle. A French bulldog with a bow on her head dropped a sharp shard of glass at Kit's feet.

"For the shaving," she said. "If you choose to set him free."

Kit dropped the rope and picked up the gleaming glass shard, sharp enough to slice the whiskers from a weasel.

"No!" Titus whimpered. "No! No! No! You can't do this to me! You can't throw me in there! I am Titus! I am your leader! He is bug-breathed alley trash! No!"

His paws left the ground as the other pets dragged him to the puddle's edge. His tail tucked between his legs, and his little gray snout whipped around, his eyes searching the crowd for a friendly face, just as Kit's had moments before.

He whimpered.

Kit dropped the shard of glass and held a paw in the air to stop them from tossing Titus into the puddle.

"A Friend to All in Need of One," he said to the terrified dog. "As the winner of this duel, I give Titus a chance to avoid his punishment!"

The crowd gasped.

"But that's not how a Dog's Duel works!" the French bulldog said.

"I am *not* a dog," Kit told her. "And by the law of Azban, the First Raccoon, I'm a friend to all in need of one." He looked Titus up and down. "Even if he doesn't deserve it."

"Young Kit"—Mr. Peebles stood on tiptoes to whisper in Kit's ear—"he would never do the same for you."

"Mercy's a gift I can give," said Kit. "So I'm giving it."

The pets let go of Titus, who slumped, sad-eyed, to the ground.

"You've defeated me," Titus said. "Take your prized food and go. Please, leave me to face my shame alone."

"You can have your shame," Kit said. "But I'm not taking your food."

"What?"

"You must!" said Mr. Peebles. "If you don't take any prize from the duel at all, then we'll have to toss him into the puddle ourselves, simply to preserve the rules. These rules have served us since the Duke of Dogs ruled all the

Flealess. We cannot let our traditions be mocked by an outsider! A Wild One at that!"

"Oh, I'll take a prize," Kit reassured the gathered pets. "I just can't carry very many cans full of food by myself, not as many as I need anyway."

"So what do you want?" Titus pleaded. His eyes darted back to the terrible puddle.

"I want your garbage," Kit said. "I want all your best garbage. The cleanest cans and the best bags. Cat food, dog food, bird food too. Any empty thing you've got."

"But our empty trash is worthless," said Titus. "Even to a Wild One like you."

"We're telling Coyote the end of a story tonight, Titus," Kit told him. "And a good story needs details. In fact, I need you to get to work on my details now."

"To work?" Titus looked terribly confused.

"Yep," said Kit. "You're going to lick every old can so clean it shines like new." Titus looked doubtful. "Of course," Kit added, "you could always get tossed in the Skunk Puddle, and I can clean the cans myself."

"No, no, no!" Titus whined. "I'll clean them! I'll clean them! But I will remember how you've shamed me, Kit. I will always remember."

"Good," said Kit. "Then maybe you'll think twice about causing me trouble."

The dog grunted, but agreed to do as he was told. "Bring me the cans!" he ordered the other Flealess as they released him. He glared at Kit. "It seems I have a lot of licking to do."

Kit nodded.

"And I've got to go," he said. "I just figured out that my story needs a few more characters."

Part III

THE BLOWOFF

Chapter Twenty-Two

THE POETRY OF FOXES

MR. Timinson taught the night's lesson as if everything were normal. He showed the students paintings of different kinds of Rumblers, some with two wheels, some with four, and some that even had eight wheels, and he explained how dangerous they were for animal folk—"as our absent friend Kit nearly showed us last night." Then he explained how best to avoid getting squashed by these cars.

"Wouldn't this lesson have been more useful *before* we ran across the road last night?" Eeni asked their teacher.

"Of course not," said Mr. Timinson. "Then how would you have figured it out for yourselves?"

Other than that one mention of Kit, Mr. Timinson acted like he didn't know what was happening back in Ankle Snap Alley, or like he knew and didn't care.

But he had also acted like he couldn't hear the students' grumbling tummies back at the Crows' Carnival until he bought them all Worms 'n' Nuts to eat. He wasn't the sort of teacher who talked about helping; he just helped.

Eeni wondered whether he was going to help now. Would Kit even let the teacher help? He'd turned down Eeni, his best friend. She was still bristling mad at Kit about that.

How could he go off on his own like he did? Why did he always think *he* had to be the hero, like *he* was the center of every story? It was exactly like a raccoon to think they were sooooo clever all on their own, like they could hold the whole world in their clever little paws.

But Kit would've been worm meat ages ago if it weren't for Eeni. He was treating her like she needed to be protected, when it was *she* who protected *him*!

She ground her tiny teeth together so hard it'd take days for them to get sharp again. Why did it bother her so much? *Friends,* Eeni figured, *are more of a nuisance than fleas in your fur.*

The lesson continued around Eeni while she silently seethed.

"Why do People make so many things that can squish us?" Matteo the mouse asked, his tiny hummingbird-feather pen quivering in his paw, poised to take notes.

"The People make things they find useful for them-selves. We are not part of their plans," Mr. Timinson answered. "They have forgotten the old stories. They build houses they think we cannot invade, and they build cages they think we cannot escape. They string wires from building to building, forgetting we can chew through them. They build and they build, but we adapt. We make highways of their wires and burrows of their gardens. Whatever they make, we can unmake."

"But . . . why do we want to unmake it?" one of the Liney sisters asked.

Eeni rolled her eyes. "Because it's *there*," she grum-bled. "Because that's what we *do*!"

"Not quite," said Mr. Timinson. "The People don't like to think about the wilds, the world that they cannot control. It scares them. As you grow up, you must remem-ber that. They seek to destroy the wild because they fear you. Their entire civilization is based on the fear of *you*." He pointed at Matteo, whose chest puffed out at the idea that the giant hairless People could fear such a fellow as him. "And they fear you! And you! And you!" Mr. Timinson pointed at Fergus the frog, and at a possum girl, at the Liney sisters, and at Dax, and then at Eeni herself. He held eye contact with her. "We go to school so we may learn never, ever to fear *them*. That is what the Moonlight Brigade did in the time when the moon was new, and that is why we study now. We are not afraid."

"We!" Eeni grunted at last. "Ha! *We* don't do anything. It's every rat for herself out in the wilds."

"Excuse me?" Mr. Timinson said.

"You think Coyote cares about any of that nonsense?" Eeni sneered. "He takes what he wants because he knows we come into the world howling and alone and we go out just as alone. We gotta get what we can while we're alive. People want to starve us and so do the other Wild Ones. Look at Shane and Flynn Blacktail. They betrayed us the first chance they got. And even Kit, our hero, ran off on his own simply to impress you, Mr. Timinson." She crossed her paws in front of her and frowned. "We're not all of one paw. We're all just one paw, and one paw alone. *Our own.*"

"Eeni's crying," one the Liney sisters pointed out.

"I am not!" Eeni answered, wiping a tear out of her eye with her tail. "My fur's still dry. If your fur's still dry, then it's not a real cry."

"Eeni, are you okay?" Mr. Timinson asked.

"She's worried about her *raccoon*," another Liney sister mocked her.

"He is not *my raccoon*," said Eeni. "And I am *not* worried about him. He'll do what he wants. Just like me." She stood up. "I'm out of here. School's not for me. I'm a loner, and I was crazy to think I'd fit in with all you tick brains."

"Don't leave yet!" a voice called out from thin air.

Everyone looked around, but couldn't see where the voice was coming from. Then a single black paw appeared over the side of the rooftop. Then another. Then a third. Suddenly, Kit's gleaming black eyes popped up above the roof's edge. He hauled himself up and landed with a flop on his belly in front of the class, out of breath.

"Kit," Eeni said. "What are you doing here? Don't you have some heroics to go do?"

"I just climbed this whole metal building to find you," Kit said, panting. "I really don't want to have to climb down again on my own. Just hear me out."

"Lovely to see you, Kit," Mr. Timinson said, as if it were perfectly normal for a raccoon to arrive on the rooftop in the middle of class.

"I get it now," said Kit. "I almost fell into a Skunk Puddle to learn it, but I get what All of One Paw really means, why the paws are together in the circle. It's not that we're all the same beneath our fur and our feathers."

Fergus croaked.

"Sorry, and our scales," Kit added. "And it's not just that we're all supposed to be the best versions of ourselves. We're nothing if we're only for ourselves. We're all different, but we're all part of the same thing. Like in music, how you don't want every note to be the same, but when all the different notes work together, you've got a song. We're the song of the wilds, and we only sing—we only *survive*—by being together."

Mr. Timinson smiled.

"So I *do* need your help," Kit said to Eeni. "I need all your help," he added, looking around at the class. "I can't do my plan on my own. *I'm* not a hero, but *we* can be."

Kit looked up and saw the bats swirling down from the sky, heading toward the school. The animals started to pack up their things to go home.

"Please," said Kit. "I've got a really good plan, but it won't work without you."

"I'll help you, Kit," said Mr. Timinson. "I was hoping you would learn when to ask for help."

"Thank you, sir," said Kit. "But I don't need your help. You're too big." He looked at the kids in his class. "I need some little heroes," he said. "The little ones are the only ones who can do this. It'll be dangerous, but who said the wild world was safe, right?" He stood on his hind legs, trying to look tall and inspiring. "So, who's with me? All of One Paw!"

No one moved.

Kit shifted from paw to paw. He looked from classmate to classmate. He looked Eeni in the eyes. Her paws were crossed, and her head was cocked.

Please, Kit mouthed.

She was still mad at him.

But, she figured, friends really were like fleas in your fur. They bothered you sometimes, but it sure was lonely without them.

"It'll be really dangerous?" she asked.

Kit nodded.

Eeni smirked. "I chew the toes off danger!" She stepped forward and stood by Kit's side. "I'm with you from howl to snap."

"From howl to snap," said Kit. "Sorry I was a tick-brain."

"You were just *acting* like a tick," she told him. "You're definitely more of a flea, though."

"Uh . . . thanks?" Kit turned back to the class. "Anyone else?"

"I'm with you too, Kit!" said Fergus, hopping by Kit's side. "We'll give that coyote something to howl about!"

"We're in too!" the moles declared.

"To danger!" Matteo the mouse shouted boldly, and scurried forward.

"To victory!" Dax darted over to Kit.

"Are you really going to let a bunch of kids fight the coyote?" one of the Liney sisters asked their teacher.

The fox took a deep breath and then recited a poem:

> *"Birds are safe in the nest,*
> *but birds are born with wings.*
> *Better to risk flying*
> *than miss out on everything."*

"Uh . . . what?" said another sister. Rats were not known for their love of poetry. A snake could count the number of great rat poets on its fingers.

"He means you can play it safe, or you can live a little!" Fergus shouted at them.

"Eeni's not going to be the *only* heroic rat tonight," the third Liney sister said, and stepped forward to join them. "We're with you!"

"We are?" said the other two.

"We are," said the first.

Pretty soon, the whole class stood by Kit's side.

As the bats flew in, Mr. Timinson looked at them proudly. "It seems you've got yourselves a brigade of your own," he told them, beaming. He pointed up. "And look, the moon's still out. I guess that makes you all the new Moonlight Brigade."

"Yeah," Kit said, smiling. He liked that. The new Moonlight Brigade. But then he looked up at the bats flying in. "The thing is, though, what we need is an air force."

After Kit had explained his plan, the class flew away with the bats, headed for home. Mr. Timinson watched them disappear into the night sky with a happy gleam in his eye, but a worried wrinkle on his brow. A loud sound of chewing broke the late-night quiet.

"It worked just as we'd hoped," the Rat King said.

"He figured it out," Mr. Timinson agreed. "Asking for help can be the bravest thing of all."

"They're all brave," the Rat King said, looming up behind the fox.

"I hope they're all smart enough to balance their bravery with brains."

"Bravery and brains are hard to keep in balance," said the Rat King. *"History is littered with the bones of folks who had too much of one, not enough of the other. But we believe they will be safe."*

Then, one voice spoke, alone in the horde. This was not the voice of the eternal Rat King, but one female voice, sweet and sad. *"He's with our daughter, after all,"* the one rat said. *"And she never lets her friends down."*

"So you do remember that she's your daughter?" the fox replied.

The Rat King answered with a hundred voices once more, *"We remember everything. It is our blessing and our curse."*

The fox looked to the cloud of bats wheeling and twirling through the dark sky on their way back to Ankle Snap Alley. The first blush of sunrise was spreading across the far horizon. The fox knew that Coyote and the Thunder River Rompers would not be far behind.

"Well," the fox said with a sigh. "I have a feeling tonight will be a night none of us will forget."

Chapter Twenty-Three

TRUST AMONG THIEVES

KIT waited alone in the dead center of Ankle Snap Alley, just as the sun was about to rise. He rubbed his eyes and plucked one of his whiskers from his snout to keep his sleepy brain focused. The quick pain woke him right up. Tired as he was, he'd need to his mind as sharp as his claws for the ordeal to come. Sharper, in fact.

All the other citizens of the alley hid behind their doors and deep in their holes. He thought he saw an eyeball peek through a crack in some shutters here, a nervous claw withdrawing behind an upturned box over there.

The tattered poster for the Dingbats' comedy show still hung on the wall outside Enrique Gallo's Fur Styling Shop and Barbería. Shredded ads for Cranston's Claw Cream were littered across the ground, and the stage from the First Frost Festival had lost one of its support posts. It sagged sideways outside the boarded-up entrance to the great stone of the Reptile Bank and Trust.

Kit strolled to the stage and climbed up. No squirrel would again wield the Great Bear's hammer in the saga of *Ratatosk*, nor would the strapping Peacock Players delight the ladybirds with their strutting. No one would *not* laugh at Declan's jokes. The stage was ruined and so was the First Frost Festival.

But all was not lost.

Kit worried for his uncle Rik, held prisoner by the Thunder River Rompers, and he worried for the Old Boss Turtle, who was a cruel gangster, but still didn't deserve to be kicked around and kidnapped. The turtle had done his best to protect the alley, as long as the alley had paid him to do it. Now that he'd failed, and failed badly, Kit figured the alley would need a new protector, or else they'd fall prey to every passing predator, from coyotes and otters to hawks and house pets.

Maybe I can take the job? Kit thought. *No,* he corrected himself. *Maybe we can do it. All of us, together. Maybe we can protect one another, my friends and I. We are the Moonlight Brigade.*

Suddenly, the hair on the back of Kit's neck prickled. His ears twitched. He sniffed and caught the scent of feathers and blood—owl smells—and then the watery smell of the gang of otters, an overpowering aroma of salt water and fish guts.

Moments after the smells hit his nose, the Thunder River Rompers burst into the alley, streaming in from both directions, a flood of angry fur, the first glimmers of sunlight shining off their glasses.

The big one, Chuffing Chaz, had angry red welts all over his face and paws.

Wasp stings.

He glared at Kit with eyes burning bright as a blazing sun. He must have opened the snout surprises. He snapped his jaw at Kit, an otter gesture that was as rude as it was terrifying. The click of his fangs made Kit shudder, and he stepped back from the front of the stage where the otters had assembled.

Behind him, the three owl sisters swooped down, heads swiveling for signs of danger. Kit was surrounded on all sides now, otters in front and owls behind.

The owls screeched so sharply it made Kit's eyeballs

jump, but at their signal, Coyote stepped forward, and behind him, the Blacktail brothers, straining with all their strength, pushed the cart that held all of Ankle Snap Alley's seeds and nuts in front of them.

Old Boss Turtle and Kit's uncle Rik were tied together on an old skateboard that was strung to the back of the cart with rough wire netting of the sort People used to keep squirrels out of their gardens. While the wire could never hope to prevent the squirrels from digging up what they wanted, it had effectively bound the turtle and the raccoon beyond any hope of escape.

"Mrmrmrmrm," Uncle Rik said when he saw Kit. He had a big stick shoved in his mouth, tied in place with a rusty bike chain. He couldn't talk through it. The turtle was in the same position, although the stick and the chain were smaller.

"Well, Kit," Coyote said, "my owls tell me you have had a busy night with your old friend Titus. I admire your pluck! Few Wild Ones have ever been inside a Flealess house, and fewer still have made it out again alive. The Blacktail brothers bet me you'd be taken by the Bagman. They lost that bet."

Shane and Flynn grunted.

"I've still got the leash I used," Kit said, holding up the leash and collar. "If you'd like to put it on like a good doggy?"

"Ha-ha!" Coyote laughed. "You are Slick of Tongue, indeed, son of Azban. Brave of Heart and Quick of Paw as well. You've got many qualities of the First Raccoon."

"And I'm Afraid of None," said Kit, trying to look defiant.

"The sun is peeking up into the sky, chasing your lovely moon away," Coyote said. "It is time to honor our deal. I know you won a Dog's Duel and I know you got your cans of food, and yet I don't see them here. You wouldn't be trying to trick old Coyote, would you? That'd be a sad song to sing, and I'd hate to have to change your tune for you."

"I've got your cans of food," said Kit. "But I'm not so crazy to have them sitting out where you could rob me again. I hid them. And I'll tell you where they're hidden, once I've got my uncle and Boss Turtle back. Then we'll trade for the seeds and nuts. But I don't make any trades when my family's held prisoner."

Coyote grinned. "Clever indeed." He nodded his head toward Shane and Flynn Blacktail. "Set loose the hostages," he grunted.

"It could be a trick!" Flynn Blacktail warned.

"You can't trust a raccoon," Shane Blacktail added.

"You two misunderstand our relationship," Coyote growled at them. "I tell you what to do, not the other way around. Power, like water, flows downhill. And you are, as you will always be, below me. Now set the hostages free!"

Shane and Flynn, grumbling, untied Uncle Rik and Old Boss Turtle.

"Sorry about all this, Boss," Shane said to the turtle.

"Don't think we ain't grateful for all you done for us," Flynn added.

"We had to do what we had to do is all," said Shane.

"I hope you can forgive us when this is over," said Flynn.

"I will forgive you," the old turtle told them. "Just as soon as I'm wearing your pelts for hats."

The brothers looked at their old boss and then at each other as if they'd each swallowed a wasp.

The turtle trudged slowly toward Kit, while Uncle Rik, once freed, ran on all fours and embraced Kit in a lung-crushing hug.

"Oh, my boy!" he cried out. "I never thought I'd see you again! I'm so glad you're okay! When they told me you'd accepted a Dog's Duel, my heart nearly turned to tar. In all our history, only one raccoon has ever defeated a dog at their own duel."

"I know," said Kit. "I read all about it in your books."

"You read my books?" Uncle Rik smiled. He seemed about as happy that his nephew had read a book as he did to be free from Coyote. His uncle was a strange and unpredictable creature, Kit decided. He was glad to have him back.

Happy tears streaked down the black fur of Uncle Rik's cheeks, and he whispered in Kit's ear, so quietly even the owls wouldn't be able to hear it. "Let's give this coyote his cans of food so he'll get out of here and leave us be."

"Oh, Uncle Rik," Kit whispered while they hugged. "If we give him whatever he wants, he'll just come back for more. He's gotta learn he can't steal from Ankle Snap Alley, once and for all."

"Kit," Uncle Rik gasped. "What have you done?"

"I'm making my mother proud," Kit answered.

"Hey, you two!" Coyote yelled. "Enough hugging and chattering like chickens. You've got your hostages back, boy. Where are my cans?"

Kit whistled loudly, and his whistle was answered by the screech of bats in the sky.

"Look up," said Kit.

A cloud of bats swarmed overhead in the red dawn sky, just like they normally would to pick up the school kids, except there were no kids waiting to go to school. All of the bats were carrying shining cans of food, wings flapping wildly with the weight they held.

Behind Kit, the owls ruffled their feathers, anxious to fly up and snatch a bat from the air. To an owl, a bat was merely a rat with wings, and the wings themselves were quite delicious.

"Have them put the food down on the stage, neatly stacked," said Coyote.

"First show me the seeds," said Kit.

"First stack the cans," said the coyote.

"Seeds," said Kit.

"Cans," said Coyote.

"Seeds!" said Kit again.

"This is a real tail turner," Coyote said. "You can't get your seeds if I can't get my cans."

"Same's true the other way," said Kit.

"Give over the cans and I'll give you the seeds. I promise," said Coyote. "Howl to snap."

"Don't say those words," Kit told him. "They mean something around here. They mean we may be no-good garbage-scrounging liars, but we're loyal to one another, from the moment we come howling into this world until the final snap of the trap that takes us out. You wouldn't understand loyalty like that if it bit you on the backside. You're a loner. Even your gang only follows you because they're afraid. They're only as loyal as autumn leaves."

"Be that as it may," said Coyote, "I've got a gang, and you don't."

Coyote let out a sharp bark, and the three owls launched themselves into the bats. Almost immediately, the swarm closed in around them. One owl slashed at Declan with her talons, but he blocked with the metal can he was holding. The talon scraped through the colorful label, but couldn't break the metal. The owl shrieked in pain, and four bats surrounded her, whacking her in the head with their cans.

The owls retreated, settling back down, bruised and angry, behind Kit.

"It's no good," one owl hooted.

"We're outnumbered," another said.

"Make your deal, Coyote," said the third. "We won't risk our beaks. We've not gotten the rats we were promised. The Rat King's gone, and we're going home. There is nothing but trouble for us in Ankle Snap Alley."

"Grrr," Coyote growled at them.

"Keep your *grrr*," an owl mocked him. "You dogs bark and snarl, but owls know whhhen a bark is hollow as a rotten tree stump. Sisters! Away!"

The owls turned, flapped their mighty wings, and flew at full speed through the cloud of bats and away from the rising sun, toward the safety of their home across the river.

"You've lost your owls," said Kit.

"But I've still got my teeth." Coyote snapped at Kit, lowering his face so close to Kit's that their noses nearly touched. "Give me my food, or I'll gnaw your bones!"

"If you gnaw my bones," said Kit, "you won't ever get

the good food that's up there. Why eat raccoon when the Fleasless food is so close? All you have to do is give me the seeds and nuts."

"Give me the food first!" Coyote shouted.

"You still don't trust me?" Kit asked, all innocence.

"You and I are both thieves, young Kit," said Coyote. "There can be no trust among thieves."

"If we can't trust each other, we'll be here all day . . . and pretty soon the People's pets will start barking at us."

"Let them bark!" Coyote laughed. "I've eaten more house pets than you've ever met in your entire life. I'm not afraid."

"You don't know much about the Fleasless, do you?" Kit asked. "You know what happens when they start barking? Their People will look outside and what will they see? Not a fearsome gang, but a coyote and some otters who shouldn't be here. And then they'll call their Bagman. I can escape up a tree, but where will you go? Where will your otters go? They're a long way from their river."

The otters whispered and worried among themselves, not looking half so ferocious as before. There wasn't a creature alive that didn't fear the Bagman. This was the last bit of Kit's gamble.

This was the Blowoff.

Coyote had to believe the story Kit was telling.

It helped that the story was true.

The sun rose higher, stretching its rays deep into the purple night and wiping away the stars. Morning was racing at them fast. Kit shivered as a brisk wind blasted against his fur.

"Fine," Coyote grunted at last. "Blacktails! Unload the cart." Shane and Flynn pushed the seed cart over toward Kit and began tossing the big sacks of stolen seeds and nuts onto the ground in front of him. It would be a mess figuring out who had lost what and how much. There would probably be a lot of fighting over it, but at least it would all be back where it belonged and all the creatures would survive another winter.

"Set them right there," Kit ordered Shane and Flynn, pointing at the ground next to the Reptile Bank and Trust.

The Blacktail brothers grumbled but did as he'd asked. Coyote watched the sacks get set down, but he didn't notice when Shane's and Flynn's thumb and foreclaws came together for an instant to form the symbol of the raccoons, and he didn't see Kit return the gesture quickly. He was too busy looking at the cans circling in the sky again.

"Kit," Coyote ordered. "Have those bats stack my cans on the cart or my boys will tear you and your uncle limb from limb. That's our deal."

Kit took a deep breath. "I'm guessing you don't have many friends," Kit said.

"What are you talking about?" Coyote snarled.

"If you knew what real friendship was," Kit continued, "you'd be wondering right about now where *my* friends were. You saw me with them when you first came to town. You saw my friend Eeni try to protect me from you, but you aren't even curious where she is?"

"Why should I care where a little white rat is?" Coyote asked. "Just give me what I came for or face my wrath!"

Kit shook his head. "You really should pay better attention. It's the little details that make a good story, and a trick is just a really good story told to a rube."

"I'm no rube, and you are—" Coyote began to object, but was cut off by Kit's loud whistle.

At the command, the bats flipped the food cans they were carrying sideways, revealing their open tops and showing that inside there wasn't a winter's supply of tasty Flealess food, but rather mice and rats, a squirrel, some moles, and a frog, all of them little schoolchildren and all of them armed for battle with rubber-band slingshots loaded with matches and sharp pebbles for firing.

"Air assault ready!" Eeni declared with confidence. Kit looked up to his friend and gave her the raccoon salute with his fingers. She was in command just where she belonged.

Chapter Twenty-Four

WASP WALLOP

I know you like music," Kit told Coyote. "You taught me this tune!" He raised a paw and shouted: "Fire at will!"

Eeni struck the match in her bow against the can, sparking its tip alight. Then she fired the flaming match straight for Coyote's face. From the open cans all around her, young rats and mice and moles rained fire down on Coyote and his gang.

The otters could hardly reach for their weapons before a lit match singed their fur. They ran for cover, shielding themselves behind trash-can lids and heaps of garbage.

"Return fire!" Coyote yelled at his gang.

Chuffing Chaz pulled out his slingshot and fired a rusty nail right for Eeni's can.

Just before it struck, the bat above turned and deflected the shot off the side of the can.

Clang!

Other shots followed, all of them bouncing harmlessly off the metal cans. The alley echoed with the sounds.

Clang! Clang! Clang!

"The cans are protecting the little fellas, Boss!" Chuffing Chaz yelled. "Can't hit so much as a whisker!"

"Then aim for the bats!" Coyote shouted back. "Drop them from the sky!"

"That's our cue, boys!" Declan yelled. "Time to scatter! Good luck, Eeni!"

"Thanks, Declan!" Eeni shouted back, bracing herself inside her can.

"Let 'em roll!" Declan shouted. He dove toward Chuffing Chaz. The big otter raised his slingshot, but just as he was about to fire, Declan released Eeni's can. It flew straight at the otter, knocking him over as it hit the ground, rolling. Other otters dove from its path. The rest of the bats rolled their cans to the ground the same way, bowling over otter after otter.

In the chaos of battle Coyote bounded for the spot where Shane and Flynn had left the seed sacks. He grabbed one in his jaws and lifted it up to haul back to the cart. No sooner had he set his paws on the piles of leaves in front of the sacks than a loud snap cracked the morning air.

"Ooowooooo!!" he howled in pain and dropped the sack of seeds again. A metal mousetrap had snapped shut on his paw. He tried to shake it off, hopping on three legs, when there was another *SNAP!*

"Owooo!" A second mousetrap snapped shut on another foot. Pretty soon he was hopping and dancing in pain.

SNAP! SNAP! SNAP!

The little metal mousetraps nipped and bit at him, and he howled in pain, rolling and dancing to get them off. It looked like his strange performance at the First Frost Festival.

"Sorry, Chief," Flynn Blacktail said, laughing.

"Gotta mind where you put your paws around here." Shane Blacktail chuckled.

"But you're on my side!" Coyote howled.

"Now, wait a whisker's width," said Shane.

"Just because it stinks don't mean it's a skunk," said Flynn.

"We're Ankle Snappers from tail to teeth," Shane said. "And when Kit made the sign of Azban at us the night you showed up, we knew we had to scheme up a way to keep you out of the fight."

"Quick of Paw and Slick of Tongue, Brave of Heart,

Afraid of None. A Friend to All in Need of One," added Flynn.

"We're all that and more," said Shane. "We weren't about to let anyone *but us* steal from our neighbors!"

"Raccoons have four paws," said Flynn. "You shouldn't watch only two."

"So we set your bags down, and set some traps down too," said Shane.

"Go get 'em, Kit!" Flynn shouted. "Our traps'll keep Coyote busy for you!"

Meanwhile, Eeni's can rolled to a stop against the Dumpster, and she crawled from it, dizzier than she thought she'd be. Suddenly, Chuffing Chaz loomed before her, covered in wasp stings.

"Oh, I see you opened our snout surprises," Eeni said.

"I told you we otters don't forget an insult," Chuffing Chaz responded. "And I've got wasps too!"

He pulled out a papery wasps' nest, the kind that could be purchased at any reliable thieves' market, and smashed it on the ground in front of Eeni. The swarm of buzzing bugs shot out in a rage, searching for the source of the disturbance.

They fixed on Eeni and charged.

"Ahh!" she yelled, diving back toward her can. One shot from Chaz's slingshot sent the can twirling away from her across the ground.

The swarm buzzed at her, stingers poised to strike.

"Come in here, Eeni!" Possum Ansel yelled, cracking open the door to his bakery and waving her frantically over with his paws.

Eeni started to run, but the wasps turned to cut her off. She'd never make it all the way in time.

Until Kit leaped to her side.

"You run for Ansel's!" he told her. "I've got this." He stopped running and picked up a broken paddle that the People used for some sort of tabletop ball game. "It's like Beetle Bagging."

"Only Beetles don't sting like wasps!" Eeni said.

"Well, then this is a new sport," Kit said, smirking at her. "A Wasp Wallop!"

Eeni stepped beside him and picked up a stick off the ground. "In that case," she said, "I can't let you have all the fun alone."

"All of One Paw," said Kit.

"All of One Paw," said Eeni.

They stood shoulder to shoulder as the swarm flew at them.

"Don't swing too early," said Kit.

"I'm more worried about too late," said Eeni.

The first wasps charged them, and Kit swung the paddle, just like at the Beetle Bagging booth, smacking two wasps away with one blow. Eeni caught one with her stick, and it careened sideways with such force its stinger stuck into a rotted wood board.

"Nice shot!"

"Only a hundred more to go!" Eeni swung again. Kit swung too. They whacked wasps sideways and back ways and up ways and down.

"You're pretty good at this," Kit said as he knocked a wasp from in front of his snout just before it stung him. "Why didn't you offer to do it at the carnival?"

"Well . . . you see . . . ," Eeni panted, then slapped another wasp away with her stick. She sent this one right at Chuffing Chaz, who yelled and ducked. Another otter tried to move around to sneak up from the side, but she whacked one more wasp in his direction and one more after that, all of them perfect shots that sent him scrambling for cover. "I kinda didn't want you to win that leash and collar."

"You WHAT?" Kit slapped two wasps straight for Chuffing Chaz, keeping the otter pinned behind a trash-can lid.

"I!" Eeni whacked another wasp. "Didn't!" *Whack!* "Want you!" *Whack!* "To!" *Whack!* "Get!" *Whack!* "Hurt!" *Whack!*

"But!" Kit replied, whacking wasps as he spoke. "I!" *Whack!* "Knew!" *Whack!* "What I!" *Whack!* "Was do-ing!" *Whack!*

"But, Kit!" *Whack!* "You didn't!" *Whack!* "Tell

me!" *Whack!* "And I'm!" *Whack!* "Your best!" *Whack!* "Friend!" *Whack!*

"I'm sorry!" Kit said. *Whack!* "Next time I have a plan!" *Whack!* "I'll let you in on it from the start!"

"You?" *Whack!* "Promise?" *Whack!*

"We're a team!" said Kit. "Howl!" *Whack!* "To snap!"

Eeni smiled. "That's the only promise I needed," she said. Then she charged at the last of the swarm, waving her stick at the rest of the wasps, sending them for Chuffing Chaz's hiding spot. Kit followed, whacking any that she missed.

"Rompers!" Chuffing Chaz yelled. "Forget this mess! Back to river! Retreat!"

He jumped from his hiding spot and ran straight out of Ankle Snap Alley, wasps stinging at his behind the whole way.

"We're coming back to you, Musky Mo!" Chaz shouted. "Ow! Ow! Ow!"

The other otters chased after him as fast as their otter paws could carry them. Their hides would be red and raw by the time they reached their river, but they'd learned their lesson: The city was no place for an otter. They'd stick to their own turf from that day forward.

"Get back here!" Coyote yelled, still trying to shake the mousetraps off himself. The Blacktail brothers stood over him, laughing.

The otters didn't come back. Coyote was alone.

Uncle Rik stepped up the coyote. "What you win with fear, you can lose with fear just as easily," he said.

Coyote growled, but covered as he was with mouse-traps, it sounded more like a whimper.

Kit and Eeni stepped toward him. Their classmates climbed from their cans. One by one, the doors around Ankle Snap Alley opened, and the rest of the residents came out. The rooster and the badger and the possum. The stray dog named Rocks and the Rabid Rascal mutts. Brevort the skunk, wide-awake now, his tail shaking, ready to spray. Feral cats joined squirrels and a flock of disheveled pigeons. The news finches gathered above.

Coyote was outnumbered, and this time, Ankle Snap Alley had *him* surrounded.

"Now, wait a moment," Coyote said, backing himself into a corner, his hackles up, his eyes darting. "You've tricked me, and I respect that. Pretty clever making me think these two raccoons were your enemies. But you're no killer, Kit. You wouldn't hurt a lone coyote who was just trying to get a meal, would you? Ain't you never been hungry? I was only doing what I had to do with winter coming on. Same as any Wild One."

"No," said Kit. "Wild Ones know there's enough for everyone out here. We may pilfer one another's pockets and raid one another's roosts, but we'd never let one another starve a winter out. Not even the Blacktail brothers. Everyone around here knows they're crooked grub-grubbing cheats," Kit explained, "but they're *our* crooked grub-grubbing cheats."

The crowd closed around Coyote. The barber's sharp rooster talon flashed in the morning sun. "I could give him a close shave?" he suggested.

"We could tie him to the tracks!" the leader of church mice declared, his robed followers holding a long length of ragged rope between them.

"We could peck his brains out!" the news finches cheered. "Peck! Peck! Peck!"

"Let's poison him!" one of the well-dressed banker geckos suggested, looking for his poison frog. Then he remembered his poison frog wasn't really poisonous and frowned.

"No," said Kit. "We *aren't* killers. We'll give him a chance to run away with his tail between his legs."

"We will?" Eeni wondered.

"We will," said Kit.

"I'll never run," Coyote told him.

"Oh, you'll run," said Kit. "Because there is one thing you definitely fear."

Kit whistled, and all of a sudden, from all the houses around Ankle Snap Alley, came a cacophony of barks and howls and hoots and meows. Every Flealess house pet in every People's house began such a ruckus that the People came rushing to their windows to see what the fuss was about.

And all of them saw Coyote.

"My guess is that the Bagman will be here soon," said Kit. "You can stay if you like, but we know where to hide in this alley and we'll do our best to hide one another. I don't think you'll find a friendly hole to hide in, though, do you?"

Coyote growled at Kit, poised to pounce, then looked to the windows, where the shapes of People pointed and stared.

"We could always tie you up and leave you here for the Bagman?" Kit suggested.

"Well played," Coyote growled. "You've out-tricked a trickster. This time. But we *will* meet again!"

"You know where to find me." Kit crossed his front paws, defiant.

"Us," said Eeni, stepping up beside him in front of Coyote's snarling mouth. "You know where to find *us*."

"All of us," said Uncle Rik, also stepping beside Kit.

"Together," said Liney sisters, stepping forward beside Eeni, paw in paw. Fergus hopped up beside them and they held his paw too.

Soon the whole alley stood beside Kit, paws, claws, and even wings crossed.

"We're ready for you," said Kit. "From howl to snap."

Coyote growled again, then turned tail and ran. He leaped the fence at the far end of the alley, yelped when he hit the ground on the other side, and limped off on his way to whatever dark wood he'd come from.

When he was gone, Uncle Rik cleared his throat. "We best all hide ourselves," he suggested. "Before the Bagman comes."

"Actually, we don't have to worry about that," said Eeni.

The other animals looked at her puzzled, then she pointed to the thick black wires that crisscrossed between all the People's houses.

Except they weren't crossed between the People's houses; they hung limp and dead off the sides.

"Our teacher told us how the People use these wires to talk to one another. That's how they call the Bagman," she explained. "Except they can't use them to call the Bagman because my friend Dax chewed through them all."

From the top of the house, Dax the squirrel poked his head up, a devious grin on his face and crumbs of black in his teeth. He also had a bald spot on his head where a wire had singed off some of his fur. Not all of the People's wires were safe to chew, after all.

"Well!" Uncle Rik puffed his chest out and looked around the alley at his neighbors, who were so rarely seen together in the sunlight. "It looks as if my nephew and his friends have saved our alley once again! The Moonlight Brigade is back!"

"Howl to snap," they all replied together.

"I guess we should sort out those seeds?" Uncle Rik suggested, but before he could turn around, all the creatures of the alley had raced for the sacks, trying to get their paws on as many seeds and nuts as they could.

"Order! Order!" the gecko banker yelled over the crowd, who proceeded to knock him down in their frenzy.

"We took a clawful of seeds for ourselves, of course," Shane told Kit.

"A nut here, a nut there," added Flynn. "Everyone paid a little, no one paid too much."

"Fair enough," said Kit, watching the other animals grunt and grumble at one another as they tried to sort out whose pouch was whose and who owed what to whom. Dimitri the hedgehog had Blue Neck Ned in a headlock, while the porcupines chased one another around the alley with their quills, calling out shenanigans.

It was messy and loud, and there was more shouting and growling than would be considered polite by decent creatures, but this was Ankle Snap Alley. They didn't *do* polite, and they were hardly decent, but one way or another, the Wild Ones kept themselves together.

"There's no place like home." Eeni smiled.

Chapter Twenty-Five

ALL OF ONE PAW

AS the animals scuffled in the morning light, Kit, Eeni, and Uncle Rik returned to the Gnarly Oak Apartments to get some well-earned rest. Possum Ansel promised to bring by some fresh acorn-and-sap-syrup cakes for breakfast when the sun went down, and the Old Boss Turtle declared that this First Frost would be forever remembered as the Frost of the Frightened Coyote.

No one paid him much attention. They all knew who the real protectors of Ankle Snap Alley were.

"The Moonlight Brigade is back!" Eeni ran circles around Kit in the hallway as she talked excitedly. "Those

Rabid Rascals can't scare folks anymore. We should tell them to take a hike! Or better yet, to do our chores! How great would it be to see the Blacktail brothers do our chores?"

"But, Eeni," Kit said, "you don't have any chores."

"Well, hmm." Eeni tapped her tail against the floor in thought. "I'll have to invent some, then! Do leaves need polishing? Can you alphabetize hairballs?"

"What you both have to do," said Uncle Rik, "is get some sleep."

Uncle Rik made up Kit's bed for him, while Kit put the scattering of books he'd used to learn about the Dog's Duel back on the shelves.

"You can read those anytime you want," said Uncle Rik. "There are lifetimes of learning in those pages."

"Thanks," said Kit, less eager to read now that his life wasn't hanging in the balance. He was really looking forward to curling up in his warm and cozy bed.

His head hadn't even hit the mossy pillow when a knock on the door pulled him up again.

"Hello, yes?" He heard Uncle Rik answer the door. "What are you all doing here . . . um . . . I'm not sure now is the best time, but . . . well . . . might I offer you some rose petal tea?"

Kit poked his head out of his room to see who had arrived. Eeni poked hers out too.

There in the entrance hall stood his teacher, Mr. Timinson, hat in hand, as well as Cawfrey the crow from the carnival.

"We're sorry to bother you after what must have been an exhausting ordeal," said Mr. Timinson. "We need to speak to Kit and Eeni."

"They've gone to bed," said Uncle Rik. "In spite of all they've done, they are still children and need their sleep. Could this wait until sunset?"

"It cannot!" cried Cawfrey the crow.

"It's okay, Uncle Rik," said Kit, stepping into the hallway. "I'm awake."

"Me too," said Eeni, stepping beside him and rubbing her eyes.

Kit couldn't see past the fox and the crow to the outside, but whatever stood in the doorway was large enough to block out the sun and cast a swarming shadow into the apartment.

"We'll wait out here," said a hundred voices speaking as one.

It was the Rat King come to pay a house call.

Eeni gasped.

"You have proven yourselves worthy above and beyond the measure of your youth. We are proud of you," the Rat King said, its voice echoing down the narrow hallway. "Both of you."

"They look surprised," said one rat voice. *"Are they surprised?"*

"You'd be surprised too, wouldn't you?" said another.

"Be quiet!" said a third. *"You're ruining the moment!"*

"We are glad, Eeni, that you did not join us," the Rat King said. "We are glad to see what a brave young rat you've become on your own."

"Yeah, well . . ." Eeni didn't have a snappy reply. She was staring at the shadow, looking for her mother among the tangle.

"You will need more of that bravery now," the Rat King added.

"Okay, can we please not speak in riddles?" said Kit. "I've had kind of a long night, you know. Tricking the Flealess, rebuilding the Moonlight Brigade, and saving the alley from Coyote and his gang? I kinda want to go to bed."

"Maybe this will wake you up?" Cawfrey said. With a flash of his claw, he flicked a small wooden disk through the air. Kit caught it and saw the symbol of the paws within paws carved into the pale tulipwood token. His mother's token.

Kit had never expected to see it again.

"We figured you'll need that more than we will," Cawfrey said.

"Thank you," Kit told him.

"Don't thank us!" Cawfrey squawked. "It's not for you to keep! It doesn't belong to you either."

"I don't understand," Kit said. "This was my mother's."

"Is," said Mr. Timinson. He rested a paw on Kit's shoulder and another on Uncle Rik's. "It *is* your mother's. How would you like to give it back to her?"

"I . . . what?" said Kit, stunned.

"Wait . . . what?" said Uncle Rik, stunned.

"Your mother is alive, Kit," Mr. Timinson repeated. "She's alive, and she's a prisoner in a place the People call a zoo. What do you think about the Moonlight Brigade, for its first mission in our wild world, coming to her rescue?"

Kit hadn't even noticed that he'd squeezed Eeni's little paw in his own, and both of them were already nodding yes together.

They didn't know what a zoo was or where or how they would break his mother out of one, but they didn't need to know that yet. They knew that they'd do it together and that together, they could do anything.

"All of One Paw," said the fox.

"All of One Paw," repeated the young leaders of the Moonlight Brigade.